# THE LION

Deep and steady, the sound rose above the winter wind. The lion listened intently. There had been four hounds on his trail originally, but only three had followed over the long chase. Now the lion knew where the fourth one was; it was on his trail and coming fast.

The tip of the lion's tail twitched angrily. He had failed to kill any hounds before because there were three.

Now there was only one.

# Lion Hound
## by Jim Kjelgaard

Illustrated by Jacob Landau

A BANTAM SKYLARK BOOK®
TORONTO • NEW YORK • LONDON • SYDNEY • AUCKLAND

## RL, 010-014

LION HOUND

*A Bantam Skylark Book / published by arrangement with
Holiday House, Inc.*

PRINTING HISTORY

*Holiday House edition published September 1955
2nd printing ......... March 1956
3rd printing .......... June 1957
7 additional printings*

*Bantam Skylark edition / February 1980
2nd printing ....... January 1981
3rd printing ...... September 1983
4th printing ....... December 1985*

ISBN 0-553-15427-3

*Published simultaneously in the United States and Canada*

PRINTED IN THE UNITED STATES OF AMERICA

CW     13  12  11  10  9  8  7  6  5

*For Debbie and Pat*

# Contents

# Lion Hound

# 1

# Snowstorm

When Johnny Torrington awoke, the autumn dawn was still two hours away. For five luxurious minutes he stretched in his warm bed, the covers pulled up to his chin while he listened to the wind blowing through the bedroom's open window. Though the wind was no colder than it had been yesterday, it seemed to have a quality now that had been lacking then.

Three weeks ago, mellow under the Indian Summer sun, bright leaves had made the rimrock country a riot of color. Then a north wind had ripped through them, sending fluttering leaves to the ground and whirling them far from their parent trees. Sometimes merely chilling and sometimes blasting cold, the north wind had blown ever since. All it had brought so far was cold rain, but now there was a definite promise of snow. Tomorrow was Saturday, and if there should be snow, Jake Kane would go up in the heights with his pack of lion hounds. Jake had promised that Johnny could go on the first hunt with him.

In his mind's eye Johnny pictured Jake's five hounds sweeping through the snow. He heard their discordant tonguing fade in the distance. He saw the snow-draped rimrock and himself listening for the hounds' frenzied tree bark. He saw a lion high in a pine and heard the crack of a rifle. The lion pitched out of the tree to land limply in the snow. . . .

The dream faded and Johnny made ready to go to school.

He sprang out of bed and raced across the floor in his bare feet. But before he closed the window he leaned out of it for a moment to draw his lungs full of crisp air and look anxiously for traces of snow. He could neither see nor feel any, but he knew it was coming because the wind promised it.

Johnny shucked his pajamas off, threw them on the bed, and dressed hurriedly. He draped a tie over his shoulder but kept his shoes in his hand as he stepped softly down the stairs. Johnny lived with his grandfather, old Allis Torrington. A renowned hunter in his day, Allis was old now and his were the ways of the old. He liked to sleep until he was ready to get up.

Johnny padded into the kitchen, lighted an oil lamp, and relaxed in the warmth from the banked fire in the big range. Two hounds, so old that they were almost toothless and with a white frosting on their dark hair, rose to greet him. They were Sounder and Pat, sole survivors of the last lion pack Allis Torrington had ever run. Old pensioners now, they slept in the kitchen whenever they chose.

Stooping to pet the two old hounds, Johnny smiled indulgently. The dogs were old, and filled with the aches and ailments of the old, but they still prowled the nearby woods and occasionally raised their ancient voices when they found the trail of a bobcat or coon. Not for a year had either of them brought anything to bay, but they were still anxious to try.

Johnny opened the door and let the two hounds out into the pre-dawn blackness. He glanced quickly at the clock on the table, noted that it was quarter past six, and dipped a panful of hot water from the stove's reservoir.

After washing, he lifted the stove lid, poked gray ashes from glowing embers, and added fresh wood. While the fire renewed its life, Johnny ducked into a cold side room and brought out a slab of home-smoked bacon. He cut thin slices, leaving four on a saucer for Allis and putting four into a skillet. As the bacon began to sputter, the coffeepot, on the back of the stove, started to steam. Johnny turned his bacon with a fork, broke two eggs in the skillet, and cut bread.

When he finished his meal, the windows were dim with approaching dawn and the cloudy sky bore out the promise of snow that had been in the wind.

Wistfully Johnny looked at the two rifles in the rack. It was always more fun to hunt than it was to attend school, but he dared not skip. His marks, while fair, were not as good as they might be and the faculty at Gatson High took a dim view of anybody who failed to attend without an excellent reason.

Johnny put more wood on the fire, turned the damper down, and let the two old hounds back in. Shivering, they went to their beds beside the stove and curled up gratefully.

Johnny scribbled a note: "Good-bye, Grand Pop. Behave yourself." He grinned as he propped the note on the table. Allis had a voice like a bull's roar, and outwardly affected a manner to go with the voice. Inwardly he was sentimental. Though he often snorted belligerent protests when Johnny called him Grand Pop, he was proud of the title and liked to be remembered.

Johnny left the dishes where they were. Allis seldom left the house for very long in cold weather and liked to have little tasks to occupy him. As Johnny donned his heavy windbreaker, he looked at his overshoes. He knew that he would be needled if he wore them to school when there wasn't any snow. But it probably would be snowing tonight and Johnny had to walk a half mile to the bus stop. He slipped his overshoes on, pulled a wool cap down over his ears, and trotted up the gravel road.

On both sides the high, colored bluffs rose up until they were silhouetted against the lightening sky.

Behind the bluffs were slides, and crumbled shale, and wild upland pastures, and creeks that spilled over ledges half a hundred feet high. But the bluffs were the most prominent feature of this land. They were seamed with fissures, lined with ledges, and honeycombed with caves that were anywhere from a few feet square to big enough for a whole house full of rooms. And to the north was a vast plateau where grew great forests of ponderosa pine.

As he trotted up the gravel road toward the highway, Johnny's mind peopled the wilderness with the creatures whose abode it was. There were mule deer, lordly elk, a few antelope, bears, coyotes, many kinds of small game. Among them, like tawny puffs of smoke, slunk the creeping mountain lions that were able to break a bull's neck and yet were so secretive. These were the big cats that Allis used to hunt and that Jake Kane hunted now. They were creatures of lore and legend, still so little known that few people really understood where the legend ended and the lore began.

Johnny looked longingly at a draw that led up into the rimrock. He pictured himself, rifle in hand, climbing that draw with Jake Kane and Jake's hounds. Then he grinned and trotted on. That was for tomorrow. Today was today. Johnny came to where the gravel road met the macadam just as the bus came into sight.

As it churned to a stop in front of him, the driver opened the door, grinning, "So you've turned sissy on us! Overshoes, yet!"

"Hi, Chuck."

Johnny stepped in, nodded to the students already in the bus, and settled down to take the ribbing he had known he would get if he wore overshoes. But he was sure he was right. The black clouds that arched the early morning sky had something besides rain in them. There would certainly be snow by tomorrow morning and probably before night.

The bus halted momentarily as Chuck applied the brakes. Johnny saw the cow elk that had been in the road, and that now moved leisurely away, looking inquiringly back at the bus. It was strange that an animal which, under ordinary circumstances, would have fled at sight of a human was not at all afraid of them when they were in a car or bus. Maybe they couldn't get the scent, or maybe they knew that cars and buses always stayed on the road and never invaded the woods. Johnny made a mental note to ask Allis's opinion on this interesting subject.

The bus stopped to take in the Barstow twins, then settled for the stiff climb out of the canyon. It halted again while a herd of mule deer scampered across the road and into the forest. Johnny watched them closely, but only because he was more interested in wild life than the others were. Wild animals in the road were routine to these youngsters who lived in the back country.

An hour and twenty minutes after it left the stop where Johnny got on, the bus rolled into Gatson and stopped at the high school. As they filed out, Johnny fell in behind Bob Carew, whose father owned a small ranch. Bob's consuming ambition was to teach English and Johnny supposed that was all right. It would hardly be a balanced world if everybody, like Johnny, wanted to become a forester.

Johnny made his way to his locker, hung his overcoat and cap inside, and hastily rid himself of the overshoes. He went to the window and looked hopefully for signs of snow before entering his home room. Cloud banks obscured the top of Gatson Peak completely. Johnny knew that the impending snow had already started up there.

All morning he made a sincere effort to pay close attention, but neither his heart nor his mind were in it. He struggled through history and English, gave himself completely to thoughts of lion hunting in the comparative freedom of a study period, narrowly escaped a reprimand in biology, ate a meal that he did not even taste at the school cafeteria, and marched with firm resolution to algebra. That was a subject that a forester should know.

As he entered the room, he glanced out of the window and saw snow falling, heavy flakes driven furiously by the north wind. Johnny tried to make out the house nearest the school, and barely saw its outline.

Two minutes later Miss Mosher, from the Principal's office, entered and spoke in a low voice to the algebra teacher. When she had gone, he faced the class.

"Torrington, Masters, Carson, Mulhaney, and Dandow are excused and will report to your bus driver."

Johnny arose along with Pete Dandow and three girls. This was routine. When heavy snow threatened, those who had to travel by bus were always excused in order to make sure that they could get home.

Johnny raced down the hall, put all except his history book in his desk, clasped the history under his arm, and ran to his locker. Bob Carew, who had the locker next to Johnny's, arrived with a big pile of books just as Johnny was shrugging into his windbreaker.

"Come on, bookworm!" said Johnny happily, turning to leave.

"I'll be there."

Pete Dandow, the Barstow twins, and Alice Larkin, whose home rooms were close to the entrance, were already at the bus when Johnny got there. The chances were good that the snow wouldn't continue, and if it didn't the roads would be cleared and they'd all be back in school Monday morning. But that was by no means a foregone conclusion. Twice last winter the rimrock road had been snowbound for four days before Chuck Jackson had again been able to get his bus through the drifts.

"Now how about those overshoes?" Johnny asked Alice Larkin.

"You think you're smart!"

Johnny grinned and dropped into a seat. Chuck Jackson, who would now have to jockey his bus through snow and get all these youngsters safely back to their homes, squinted worriedly at the school.

"Where in blazes are the rest of them?"

"Don't worry, Chuck," said Pete Dandow. "If this antique ark of yours gets stuck in a drift, we'll just pick it up and carry it. Not so sure it wouldn't be faster at that."

"Ha, ha," gritted Chuck. "We have a humorist in our midst."

The others came until all except Bob Carew were there. Chuck fidgeted in his seat, and the rest set up a chant.

"We want Bob! We want Bob! We—"

He came at last, after all but one of the other buses had left. There was a pile of books under his arm and a look of unhappy resignation on his face. Chuck gunned the motor, the bus crawled cautiously out into the street, and the wipers made squeaky little noises as they pushed fluffy snow from the windshield.

Johnny looked happily out the window. The autumn landscape of this morning had become a winter fastness. Snow covered the meadows, clung to the evergreen branches, and was piling up on the road. Dimly ahead of them Johnny saw fast-filling tracks of a car that had already gone through.

Chuck kept his bus at little more than a crawl. When he came to the hairpin turns leading down into the canyon, he eased around them in second gear. They reached the Barstow's without mishap, then Johnny's stop.

He grinned and waved as the bus went on. Naturally, he told himself conscientiously, nobody should want to get out of school. But the storm had ended formal education this week, and that was that. Through the four inches of snow he struck happily down the half mile of gravel that led to his grandfather's house. His blood raced, and for sheer pleasure he went to one side and leaped a fallen tree. Then he became more cautious, and went on slowly.

Wild creatures often started down from the heights with the first snow. Just ahead was a grove of wild apple trees where Johnny had often seen deer and elk, and he wanted to find out if any were there now.

The soft snow made silent walking. But deer and elk were quick to notice moving objects, and when Johnny came near the glade where the apple trees grew he slunk behind a pine. Keeping in line with the next one, he continued to approach the apple trees. From the sheltering trunk of the last big pine he peered at the wild orchard.

He was a little surprised to see nothing. Deer or elk should have been there, waiting for the next apple to fall or rearing on their hind legs to pluck the gnarled, frozen fruit. Puzzled, he scanned the snow for tracks. He saw none, so there had been no other passer-by to frighten the animals. Maybe there hadn't been enough snow to drive them out of the heights.

Then Johnny stood at rigid attention.

In the pines beyond the apple trees he had seen something move. It was nothing he could see clearly or identify; only a flash of tawny-brown color that appeared and disappeared. Johnny stood very quietly behind the pine, hoping that whatever he had seen would show itself more clearly. When it did not, he stepped out from behind the tree.

He saw it clearly now, framed in a little opening between two trees. Then it was gone. It was a huge mountain lion, the biggest Johnny had ever seen. He stood still and tried to think coolly.

Lions had been known to attack people; both Jake Kane and his grandfather had told him that. But such attacks were isolated instances, and usually any lion that attacked a person was driven to it only by starvation. Johnny had seen the lion clearly and it had looked anything but starved.

He moved cautiously to a dead, fallen pine, and tried to look in all directions at once while he probed with his foot for a stout branch. He picked one up, leaned it at an angle against the trunk, and jumped on it to break off a three-foot club. Quickly he stooped to take the club in his hands, then moved into an opening where there was room to swing.

Lions didn't usually attack people, but Johnny had heard that they often followed them. A lion's outstanding characteristic is an overwhelming curiosity about anything and everything, and without showing themselves they would sometimes trail a person for miles. Johnny shivered at the prospect of being trailed by a lion the size of this one.

When he went on down the snow-covered road he kept to the center, as far as possible from the brush and trees on either side. He leaped like a startled deer when there was a sudden noise beside him. But it was only an overweight of snow falling from a spruce branch.

He came to a place where the larger trees had been cut and little spruces had grown up in their wake. Not yet as tall as Johnny, the little trees were full-needled and very thick. Johnny edged cautiously past, then halted again.

He could see and hear nothing, yet he was sure that one of the little trees had moved, as though a heavy body had brushed against it. Suddenly he was overcome by a wild impulse to carry the fight to the enemy, and sprang forward, brandishing his club. A wild shriek burst from his lips.

"Hi-eee!"

Blindly he crashed into the little trees and felt them whip his face. Then he stopped short.

Fresh in the new snow were the paw marks of a huge lion. Johnny felt the hair on the back of his neck tingle, and he looked fearfully about at the enclosing evergreens. Awareness of the insane thing he had done surged over him, and he beat a hasty retreat back to the open road. He still walked slowly, trying to see everything, and only when he smelled wood smoke and saw his grandfather's house did he break into a run. As he burst through the door, his grandfather looked up in surprise.

"What's the matter, boy?"

"A lion followed me down the road!" Johnny gasped.

"A lion? You sure?"

"I saw him once and his tracks are still there!"

"How close did he come to you?"

"When I passed those little spruces he was within thirty feet."

"Do you think he aimed to tackle you?"

Johnny shook his head. "I thought so then, but I'm not so sure now. It's different when you're out on the road with only a club. Maybe he was just following me."

"Could be," Allis agreed, "but it don't sound likely. Lions that follow people don't usually come that close. Let's shag back up there."

"Good."

Johnny went to his room, took off his school clothes, and got into his hunting togs. He pulled rubber pacs on over wool socks, and took his rifle from its rack. The two old hounds looked sadly at them when they left the house. They wanted to go too, but knew they were too old now for strenuous hunting.

As he strode back up the road with his grandfather beside him, Johnny's fear was replaced by confidence. He had a rifle and he knew how to shoot it. Where he had feared the lion would come, now he hoped it would. Johnny led Allis to the little evergreens and followed his own tracks inside. The old man stooped carefully to examine the lion tracks in the snow. When he straightened, there was doubt in his eyes.

"I don't know," he muttered. "I can't tell you what that lion aimed to do and as far as I know he didn't know neither. But he sure is big and it's not healthy to have him here." The old man glanced at the darkening sky. "It's sort of late to set hounds on his trail today, but there's always tomorrow. After supper you go down and tell Jake Kane about it."

# 2

# The Lion

The lion's mind was filled with memories and his heart with hate.

He was full-grown now, a supple, sinewy creature at the very height of his powers and in the fullness of his life. He weighed well over two hundred pounds. Only in early Indian days, when game was everywhere in profusion, had bigger mountain lions roamed the rimrock. They had grown larger then because there had been an abundance of food and because hound packs, unknown until the white men brought them, had not hunted lions over the colored bluffs and rises.

This lion had also had all the food he could eat, but much of it was not food that he had hunted. Nor had his life pattern been that of any other lion on the rim.

He had been the first cub of a sleek young lioness who had prowled far and wide to find a safe den high on the side of a towering mountain. There he had been born, a squirming little spotted cub that might have nestled with room to spare in Jake Kane's cupped hands. But every day, and almost every hour, he grew bigger. Having only one cub, and finding good hunting, his mother had given him all the milk he could use.

Gradually he became more independent. It had become his consuming ambition to catch a deer, as he had seen his mother do, and he was forever stalking them. But his hunting technique was far short of perfection. He was too eager, and he either betrayed himself by some ill-timed move or started his rush too soon. Though he did catch a couple of rabbits, and numberless grasshoppers, it was early autumn before he pulled down his first live deer and that was accidental.

The lioness had gone on her stalk, which was familiar routine now. The cub heard the startled deer in wild flight when she rushed them. Then a fawn, fleeing without looking where it was going, almost overran the cub. He had only to meet it head-on and bear it down while the fawn rolled helplessly on its side.

It was a lucky encounter for the cub. A full-grown deer might have killed him, but the fawn was as inexperienced as its attacker. The cub imbedded all four taloned feet firmly in the little deer and his strong jaws sought the backbone. He bit as hard as he could, and when his teeth met through the spinal column the fawn lay still.

When the lioness, who had missed her strike, came back to the cub, he was crouched over his kill, growling at her. Angered, she took all the fight out of him with one swipe of her paw and the cub and mother fed side by side. But he had learned.

Snow fell, and the pair remained together as they prowled the wilderness. Sometimes they ate well and sometimes they went hungry, for the deer upon which they depended for the bulk of their food were neither as plentiful nor as incautious as they had been during the summer. With the approach of winter, many of the deer had gone into the lowlands and the lioness was reluctant to follow them there.

Hunger finally drove her to it, but she changed her hunting methods radically and the cub could not at first understand this. While living in the heights, they had gone where they pleased when they pleased. Here the lioness would hunt only at night. She was careful to avoid the ranches and the scattered homes, and kept strictly to the thickets where deer herds would winter through. But there were many more deer here and the lions' bellies were usually filled.

One day, after they had fed and were resting in a thicket, the lioness raised her sleek head. Because he was accustomed to doing exactly as she did, the cub looked where she was looking. The thicket was on a canyon's rim, and on the other side of the canyon walked a creature such as the cub had never seen before. It seemed a slow and plodding thing, with no harm in it, or even much of interest. The cub had seen his first man.

When it came, disaster was sudden.

The lioness had killed a deer during the night, and she and the cub had fed well. With daylight they entered a thicket about a half mile from the kill and curled up to rest. All morning they were undisturbed, but when the sun slanted past high noon the cub heard a sound which he had never heard before.

It was a mournful, rolling noise, and somehow terrifying; for the cub felt the hairs on his neck prickle. He did not know that he was hearing the bay of a hound on cold scent, but he did know that the sound originated very near the kill his mother had made last night.

Without hesitation the lioness slipped out the opposite side of the thicket, and began to run, the cub following. They did not run fast because, though lions are capable of amazing speed for a distance of a few yards, they cannot run very fast for very long. They loped along as best as they could, while behind them the uncertain baying of the hound sent echoes back from distant heights.

Suddenly the hound's baying was no longer sporadic, but sharp, eager, steady. He had found the thicket where the lioness and her cub had rested, and had hot scent now. The tonguing of a second dog mingled with that of the first.

The lioness ran faster, and there was an air of desperate fear about her now that communicated itself to the cub. Never before had he known his mother to be afraid of anything, and the certain fear that he could now sense gave added speed to his own feet.

The tonguing hounds sounded nearer and nearer, but when his mother whipped around with her back to a big tree, the cub ran blindly on. He did not know where he was going, but only that he must go. There was nothing that could have made him stop.

He heard the running hounds halt, their steady tonguing coming only from the place where his mother had stopped. One of the hounds voiced a high-pitched shriek of agony, then only one continued to tongue. After a few moments that one screamed, too.

The cub heard the blast of a rifle and then all was silence.

He did not stop because he was too terrified, and that was his salvation. Both dogs were dead, disemboweled by the lioness, and the man who shot her could not overtake the laboring cub alone.

When the cub finally did stop, too winded to run another step, he was miles from the place where his mother had made her stand against the dogs. He was still frightened and very worried, for never before had he been alone. But not for any reason would he go back. His mother, he thought, would join him here.

The cub whimpered lonesomely to himself, as he sought the shelter of an evergreen thicket. The long run had exhausted him completely, and though he was hungry, he was too tired to look for any food. He lay down beneath the evergreens and slept.

When he awakened he was still bewildered and worried because his mother was not with him, but returning to look for her was too terrifying a prospect. The dogs might be there. Starting out to hunt, the cub found and made a clumsy rush at a herd of deer. They avoided him easily, as did all the others he stalked that day and night. Three days passed before the cub fed, and then luck directed him once more.

During the hunting season, an unskilled hunter had shot at a handsome buck, but only wounded it. The buck ran a long way before its strength began to fail. Then it weakened fast, and almost anything could have pulled it down when the cub stumbled across it. The cub stayed near his kill until it was all eaten, then started out again.

At first his luck was bad and he knew more hunger. Then he found the kill of another lion, fed at it, and hastily ran away, sensing that he was trespassing and would be punished if caught.

The cub had more luck in an area where hunters had killed several deer and left their offal in the snow.

It was cold and frozen, and not at all what he liked, but it sustained life. Then, little by little, forced by necessity, his hunting skill improved. Though he still missed a good many strikes at deer, he made enough kills so that he did not grow thin or too weak to fight the bitter weather. By mid-winter he was a fairly skilled hunter.

Then the hounds came again.

The cub was lying up on a rocky ledge, trying to absorb such warmth as could be found in the winter sun, when he heard them begin to tongue near a kill he had left the previous night. Immediately he knew panic. This was the second time he had heard hounds, and as far as he knew there was no greater danger. In long, springing leaps he sped away over the snow, and as before he paid little attention to where he was going. His sole idea was to put distance between the hounds and himself.

He heard their desultory cold trail barks change to eager yelling as they came to the ledge where he had lain up. Desperately he tried to increase his pace and succeeded only in running himself nearly breathless. The cub leaped at the trunk of a pine, drew himself up, climbed halfway to the top, and tried to flatten himself against the tree.

He heard the hounds come, and because he was born curious he could not resist peeking around the tree trunk at them. Four black and tan brutes, they gathered beneath the tree and made the air hideous with their yelling while they leaped upward and fell back. The cub breathed a little easier. He hadn't been sure he'd be safe even in a tree, but obviously the hounds couldn't climb trees.

Twenty minutes later three men arrived and the cub peered wonderingly at them. He'd had almost nothing to do with men aside from having seen one across a canyon and running across their tracks now and again. But there had been nothing in his experience to prove that men were dangerous; the dogs seemed far more to be feared.

"It's just a cub!" one of the men yelled. "Tie up the dogs and we'll take him alive!"

Amazed, the cub watched two of the men catch the dogs and tie them to trees. He scanned the men carefully, and had a first uneasy premonition that he had underestimated them. But even though he was frightened he was still curious enough to want to see for himself what was going on.

A coil of rope around his shoulder, one of the men began climbing the tree. The cub started up the trunk, then changed his mind and crawled out on a branch. But when the branch swayed and bent beneath his weight, he became afraid he would fall and stopped to hold on with all four paws. Instinctively he parted his jaws in a snarl. To his great relief the climbing man did not come out on the branch at all, but continued up the trunk. The cub shifted nervous eyes from the chained dogs to the men on the ground, and back to the man in the tree.

The climbing man was above him now, bracing his feet against a branch and resting his back on the trunk. The coil of rope was in his hands, and he swung a loop. The cub saw it coming. He spat and tried to lash at it with a front paw, but when he did the branch on which he crouched swayed alarmingly and he had to give all his attention just to holding on. The loop settled over his head and tightened about his neck. The cub was jerked from his perch.

He wriggled his body, waved his paws, and above all tried to draw breath. But though he could wriggle, his whole weight hung on the rope around his neck, choking him. His tongue dangled out and his head pounded. For a moment or two he was unconscious.

Then, finally, he was stretched on the snow with his paws tied together and a stick clamped between his jaws. Helpless, he could do little except roll his eyes. He looked in turn at each of the three men, and at the hounds. His bound paws were tied to a long green pole and the cub was suspended, head downward, while two of the men supported the pole on their shoulders. The third led the leashed dogs.

The cub's only conscious emotion was overwhelming fear, but beneath the fear was hate. His paws were bound so tightly that they hurt him, and the stick in his jaws squeezed a part of his tongue against a sharp tooth. The hatred he was to feel toward all men was born in that moment.

For an hour and a half the men carrying him plodded through the snow, stopping occasionally to put their burden down and rest. They reached a highway, and the cub was unceremoniously dumped into the back of a pickup truck. The truck was run into an unheated garage, and the cub left there all night long.

Early the next morning his journey was resumed. Far down the highway he was taken, out of the wilderness where he had been born and into settled country. At first the cub shivered every time they passed another car, then he became used to them and did not flinch any more. Even the rumble of heavy trucks did not disturb him unduly. Finally the truck stopped, and the driver got out.

"I've got a lion for you, Tom," he said.

"Good," a strange voice answered. "Let's see him."

The cub was lifted out of the truck and could look about him. There was a building nearby such as he had never seen before, and a couple of automobiles parked in front of it. A ring of curious people gathered. The cub could not know that he had been brought to a filling station, nor read the sign which explained why he had been brought here: STOP! LOOK AT THE LIVE MOUNTAIN LION!

The cub knew only that there were smells here which he did not like because they hurt his nostrils, and too many of the man-creatures which he hated. He was carried to a kennel, where a strong leather collar attached to a chain was strapped about his neck. Then the man who had brought him here cut the ropes that bound his paws and held the stick in his jaws. The man leaped clear.

He was in no danger. The cub wanted only to get out of sight and leaped at once into the kennel, the only hiding place he could see. For the first time since his capture he knew some measure of comfort. There had been another lion here before him, and judging by the scent, it had been a very old beast. The cub could not know that it had died, or that he was taking its place as an attraction for the filling station.

Not until night, when everything was quiet, did he venture out of the kennel. He sniffed suspiciously at a bowl of horse meat that had been placed within his reach, and licked at it. But he was still too nervous and excited to be hungry. He padded as far as the chain would let him go and looked longingly at a cluster of pines across the road. He could smell them too, the only link with the wilderness home he loved so well.

The next morning he was in the kennel when he heard a car stop and the voices of people. He saw them bending and peering in the door, and cowered in the farthest corner. Then the filling station owner brought a long pole with a hook on the end. He hooked a link of the chain and dragged the cub out into the open, bruising the lion's side against the kennel door. While the man held him, another man slid a board over the kennel door so the cub could not get back in.

The people backed away. The cub slunk around the corner of his kennel and lay uneasily while his side throbbed and hurt him. Fear still ruled him, but mingled with it was a rising resentment. Even while he wished there was some place he might hide, the end of the cub's tail twitched menacingly.

It took him a month to become adjusted, so that he would eat every night and of his own accord venture out of the kennel by day. He had already discovered, after several desperate attempts while the friendly night shielded him, that the chain and collar could not be broken, so he had stopped trying. He had also found that, though he detested everything about the place, apparently he was meant to come to no harm here.

The cub lay in front or on top of the kennel and blinked what appeared to be sleepy eyes at the many people who came to stare at him. The people could not have been more mistaken. While they looked at him, the cub studied them. He knew they were dangerous because people had made him a captive, but they had their weak points, too.

Spring came and summer followed and winter came again, and still the cub lay near the kennel watching people, and studying their habits. Because he always had plenty to eat, the cub grew as no wild lion can hope to grow.

Every night, after the filling station was closed and there were few cars on the highway, the lion stood before his kennel and stared at the pines across the road. When he did he became tense and alive, and his eyes were anything but sleepy. He never lost the fierce desire to be free of his chain and back in the wilderness, but not until he had been a captive for almost three years did his chance come.

The summer sun was hot in the sky one day and the lion was dozing in front of the kennel when a big blue car stopped at the filling station. There was a man and woman in the front seat, and a big black and tan dog in the back. Almost before the car stopped the dog had leaped through a window and was rushing at the lion.

No longer a fearful cub, but fully grown, the big lion waited, crouched and snarling. The dog leaped toward him, and the lion waited until it was impossible for the dog to get back to safety. Then he slapped a front paw to either side of the dog's head, bit through its brain, and the fight was over almost before it started.

The lion drew back to get more slack in his chain for, brandishing a thermos bottle, the man was shrieking and rushing at him now. There was a shouted warning from the filling station's owner, and the hysterical tourist stopped just short of any place the chained lion could reach.

Angered, he leaped anyhow. He went up and out, feeling the chain tighten behind him as he sprang.

The chain held, but the leather collar was now old and worn. The collar snapped, and the lion bore the white-faced tourist down. He would have killed him there had he not instantly realized that the freedom he longed for was now his. The lion sprang across the highway into the pines.

When he came to the end of the pines, he crossed a field and found himself in a forest of hardwoods. At the far side of the forest he slowed to a walk, and that night he feasted on a sheep which he took easily from a bleating flock. Fortunately for him, neither the farmer nor the filling station owner thought of putting an experienced lion hunter with trained hounds on his trail, and the volunteer hunters were soon left far behind.

The lion traveled on, but after the first day he moved only at night and lay up when the sun shone. His captivity had taught him much, and among the things he had learned was the fact that humans can see or sense little in the dark. At night he felt perfectly safe, and often walked within feet of houses in his path. Once, after midnight, he padded right through a village.

Twice on his long journey he was attacked by farm dogs that snarled out at him. They were mere annoyances. Though the lion had learned by experience that he must never again run up a tree when dogs were on his trail, he was not afraid of any one dog. Leaving the dogs where he killed them, the lion continued his journey. He did not like this country and would not stay in it.

He took his food where he found it: sheep, calves, and once a horse. By this time he was far enough from the filling station so that news of his escape had not preceded him, and the killings were ascribed to packs of wild dogs which infested the country.

Two weeks after his escape, the lion stalked and killed his first deer. He made no mistakes in the stalk and he did not miss the final strike. His early hunting training had come back to him, the journey had toughened him, and he was no cub now, but a fully mature mountain lion. But, even though there were deer in it, this country was still too settled for his taste. He went on until he reached the rimrock, and there he was content to stay.

He had learned a great deal about men and their ways, and he understood how to use that knowledge. A sullen, dangerous beast, he was prepared to make the rimrock his kingdom, to hold it against all challengers, and to raid wherever he wished.

# 3

# The Red Pup

Johnny took a second helping of Allis's flaky apple pie, sighed contentedly, and pushed his plate back on the table. When he had first discovered that the lion was following him he had been tense and nervous, but that feeling had passed. Now he was satisfied that the beast had been merely curious, and had come so close because it thought itself unseen. It had retreated fast enough when Johnny rushed it with his club and yelled.

Johnny grinned. "That lion and I must have both looked foolish when I ran at him shrieking like a banshee."

Allis shook his head. "It mightn't have been so funny if you hadn't. A lion's nerves are set on a hair trigger. If he did aim to tackle you, yelling thataway could have changed his mind."

"Do you think he really intended to attack me?"

"I didn't say that. I said he might have. I've lived in

these woods more than seventy years, and I still can't tell what any critter'll do. Neither can any other man. Not even Jake Kane, and that's his business."

"I don't believe he meant anything."

Allis snorted. "When I was your age I knew twice as much as I do now, too. Take your rifle and Pat or Sounder when you go down to Jake's. And pack a light, naturally."

"Pat or Sounder couldn't help."

"Either one can let you know if that cat comes close again; any dog knows six times as much about what's around as any man. You take a hound."

"Yes, Grand Pop."

"And don't call me Grand Pop!"

"All right, Grand Pop," Johnny grinned.

He rose to get his hunting jacket, hung an electric torch on his belt, took his rifle from its rack, and snapped a short leash onto Old Sounder's collar. Now that he had had a chance to think it over, with no lion near, it all seemed pretty silly. Johnny glanced covertly at his grandfather. He didn't know, nor did Allis, whether he was seventy-eight or eighty-three. But he was pretty old and it was just as well to humor him. Besides, Sounder would enjoy the walk.

Johnny found that the snow had lessened to a light fall and that there was little wind stirring. But it was pitch dark after the lighted room, and Johnny suddenly realized that he was grateful for Sounder's company.

A quarter of a mile down the road they came to Jake Kane's house.

It was built back off the road, in a cluster of pines, because that's the way Jake wanted it. He had been born in a sheep camp and had spent most of his life in the back country. In a modern age, with streamlined cars on the hard-surfaced road and jet planes overhead, Jake still preferred the odor of horse flesh to the stench of gasoline.

Jake's hound pack, chained to separate kennels, set up a thunderous baying when Johnny approached. By their voices he identified Major, Doe, Rowdy, and Flutter. Sally, the fifth member of Jake's pack, slept inside the house with her three puppies. Johnny reached down to touch Sounder reassuringly, but the old hound was quiet. In his day Sounder had had his share of battles. But that was all behind him now and he looked down, from the dignity of his years, at the petty squabbles of younger dogs.

The door opened and Jake Kane stood framed in a rectangle of yellow light.

"Who's there?" he called.

"Johnny Torrington."

"Come on in, Johnny."

Jake Kane was not tall, about five feet eight. Black hair interlaced with gray streaks framed a weather-beaten face of which piercing black eyes were the outstanding feature. Jake was fifty-five now and looked older, with more than forty years of hunting behind him. Wiry of frame, there was something about him that reminded Johnny of a storm-lashed and weather-beaten tree.

"I figured you'd be down, with this snow," Jake said. "And you're right; I'm goin' out in the mornin'."

Sounder stretched out near the stove and sighed blissfully. Three two-month-old puppies, one red and two blue-ticked, tumbled out of a box at the rear of the room and looked inquisitively at Sounder. Then the two blueticks raced eagerly up to Johnny and began to play with his boot laces. But the red pup hung back.

"Where are you heading for, Jake?" Johnny asked, watching the red pup.

"Haven't decided. The deer will be down and the lions will follow them. Most any place where you'd find a lot of deer you'd stand a good chance of jumpin' a lion tomorrow."

"You won't have to go very far to find a track. There's a big lion prowling right at the end of the road."

"So?"

Johnny told of seeing the lion, and of being followed by it, while Jake listened attentively. Sounder snarled and snapped as one of the puppies took hold of his ear and began to pull on it. Thus warned, the three puppies began a rollicking race around the room. But though the blueticks did not hesitate to brush past Johnny, he noticed that the red pup kept his distance.

"You say that you saw this lion?" Jake asked incredulously.

"Once, for maybe a second. He didn't stay around long."

"It's an odd thing he'd let himself be seen or stay around at all. I never knew a lion to show itself when there was a man around, less'n maybe it was a fool cub."

"This was no cub. It's the biggest lion I ever saw."

"What'd Allis say?"

"He doesn't know either. He said he couldn't tell what the lion intended to do, and neither could anyone else."

"He's right," Jake agreed. "I don't believe, though, that you were in any danger. My guess is that the lion was just almighty curious as to who you were and what you wanted, though I still can't figure his comin' so close or showin' himself. Maybe that lion's a mean old renegade who don't like people and aims to show it. Anyhow, he'll be a good one to get rid of fast. We'll see what we can do about him tomorrow."

The three puppies raced around the room, the two blueticks hot on the trail of their red brother. They caught and scrambled over him, voicing puppyish snarls as one laid hold of the red puppy's rear leg and the other tackled his front. Straining in opposite directions, they stretched him between them on the floor.

Then, suddenly, the red puppy was on his feet and scrambling over his brothers. One gave a shrill squeal of protest as his dangling ear was pinched between needle-sharp teeth, and pulled violently away.

As though he were suddenly bored with the whole proceeding, the red puppy sat down on the floor and yawned deliberately. The other two circled warily. They had learned their lesson and would be more cautious about attacking next time. Puppy though he was, the red one had taught them respect.

"Likely looking pup," Johnny said.

Jake shrugged. "They're too young to tell much about 'em yet. Some of the best lookers turn out to be the worst dubs when you get 'em on a track. But that red one does seem to have a lot of gimp."

"What's his name?"

"Haven't got around to a name yet."

"Well," Johnny grinned, "he may not turn out to be as good as your Major, but I'll bet he makes a good buck private."

Jack slapped his knee. "You've named him. We'll call him Buck, and see how he takes to basic trainin'."

Johnny extended a hand and snapped his fingers. "Come on. Come on over here, Buck."

The two bluetick puppies galloped over immediately and threw themselves at Johnny's hand. The red pup only circled cautiously. There was nothing hostile in his manner but neither was there any friendliness. Jake chuckled.

"No use. He won't come to anybody except me. But you sure tagged him."

The two blueticks went back to playing and Johnny looked admiringly at the red pup. As Jake had said, he was still too young to know what he would be when he grew up. But there was a certain air of self-assurance about him, and he had one almost priceless asset. He was not just anybody's dog but would always cling to one man and had already chosen Jake as that man.

"Where's Sally?" Johnny asked.

"I let her out for a run. She should be back by now."

Jake got up and opened the door, but there was no waiting hound outside. Jake waited a moment, whistled into the darkness, and closed the door again.

"Reckon she'll be back when she gets around to it. Can't blame her for wantin' to get away from these pups."

"They are pretty lively," Johnny agreed.

Outside, the hounds began to bay again and their voices rose to a frenzied crescendo. There came quick, thudding noises as they threw themselves against their chains and were brought up short by them. Then came another call in the night.

It was a rising, almost plaintive sound, pitched high enough so that it could be heard above the sound of the wind and the yelling dogs. There was something imperative about it, too. The creature from which the sound originated wanted something, and had no intention of being denied. Jake and Johnny grinned at each other, and Jake went to the door again.

Both knew what had made the noise. A big, tough, old house cat, appropriately named Old Nick, ranged up and down the length of the canyon. Everybody knew him, and though the region was not one where cats commanded a great deal of admiration, everybody respected this one. If Old Nick had nothing else to recommend him, he had resourcefulness, undoubted courage, and a character all his own.

An unscrupulous pirate, Old Nick was always competing for a livelihood with beasts bigger and stronger than himself. Every hound in the valley, and every hound pack, had chased him. He had never been caught, and Old Nick really seemed to like to match wits with dogs. Three times he had deliberately shown himself to Jake's hounds when it seemed that there could be no escape. But Old Nick had always gotten away, to sit in a tree or on a rock ledge while the frustrated dogs roared beneath him.

It was suspected that, in addition to whatever he caught in the wilderness, Old Nick had a soft tooth for young poultry. But nobody had ever caught him actually raiding a poultry yard. He was a wanderer who might disappear for weeks at a time, then return and take up residence at whichever house he had decided to favor with his presence. Now, having walked brazenly past hounds which he knew very well were chained, he was at Jake's door asking shelter from the storm.

Jake opened the door only part way, and in a sifting of snow Old Nick entered. The battle-scarred old cat walked to the center of the floor, sat down, and began grooming himself.

Jake whistled softly. "He really takes over when he comes in, don't he?"

Jake had hunted and killed too many cats of all kinds to have any real affection for any of them, but he couldn't help respecting this one. Half again as big as most house cats, Old Nick was a sadly battered renegade. His right ear had been sacrificed in some forgotten battle of long ago, and he had only a stub of a tail. But there was something regal in the haughty way he ignored the other occupants of the room, as though it were his, and the others the intruders. Sensing this, Old Sounder raised his head, glared balefully at the cat, and went back to sleep again.

Jake, who would feed any hungry thing that came to his door, started toward the cupboard to see what he could find there.

"Look at the pups," Johnny called.

The two blueticks raised up in their box, then went back to sleep again. But Buck stood on the floor, all four feet braced, looking belligerently at the cat. A ridiculous puppyish growl bubbled in the red pup's chest as he came forward.

Johnny had a sudden vision of old Major or Sally, facing a cornered lion. But this would be no even contest; Old Nick would kill this brash young puppy in seconds, and was perfectly willing to do it. Johnny's eyes moved nervously from the pup to the cat.

Old Nick remained where he was, washing his fur. His eyes were on the red puppy, and they were contemptuous. Old Nick had faced, and fought, hard and dangerous enemies. This silly puppy was hardly worth the ruffling of his fur.

As the puppy stalked forward, Old Nick left the floor and sprang before either Jake or Johnny could move. His front paws were extended, ready to strike. A split second behind Old Nick, Jake leaped forward with a shout.

Though the cat landed where Buck had been, the red puppy was no longer there. Unable to whirl or dodge as a mature hound might have, he had simply rolled out of danger. Two bright flecks of blood showed where the cat's claws had pierced his puppy skin.

The pup was to his feet, entirely willing to continue the battle, when Jake swooped and plucked him from the floor.

"You little fool," he said gruffly. "Want to get yourself killed before you've ever had a chance to grow up?"

For all his harsh words, the old lion hunter was proud of the pup. For almost forty years he had raised and followed good hounds. But never before had he seen hunting and fighting instinct so strong in a pup so young. Still holding the struggling puppy, Jake opened the door.

"Come on, Nick," he said. "Find yourself another bunk for the night."

Still contemptuous, Old Nick walked out the door, and Jake put the pup down. Buck snuffled busily at the scent Old Nick had left. He followed to the door and came back again, casting in a little circle as though he might have missed something.

"Darned if he isn't trailing!" Johnny said.

"He's got it all right," Jake agreed.

The two blueticks stirred restlessly in their box and whined. The red pup went back to his brothers, and the three set up a plaintive whimpering.

"That doggone Sally ought to come back and feed her babies," Jake grumbled. "Guess I'd better go out and find her. She may be in trouble."

"I'll go with you," Johnny offered.

Jake put in place the board that kept the puppies from leaving their box. As the men put on their hats and jackets, and Johnny caught up his rifle, Sounder looked up inquiringly.

"He's pretty old," Jake said. "We'll take Major."

"Stay, Sounder," Johnny said gently.

The old hound went gratefully back to sleep beside the stove and Jake and Johnny stepped out into the lightly falling snow. The hounds rattled to the ends of their chains and sat hopefully waiting. When Jake unchained only Major, the rest of them whined dismally.

Major was the best of the Kane hounds. Like the others, he was gaunt and slat-ribbed, lean of paunch, and strong of chest. Though it could be seen only in a strong light or when they turned their heads a certain way, there was about the eyes and muzzles of all Kane hounds a faint suggestion of bristle. Somewhere back in their ancestry was the blood of fighting terriers. No judge in any dog show would have recognized them as pure-bred, or even known exactly where to place them. But any of a hundred hunters, men who knew the back trails and the beasts that frequented them, would have known any of Jake's dogs as a Kane hound and given two months' pay for it.

Jake stood uncertainly while the falling snow flew softly against their faces. The missing mother of the pups could be anywhere at all, and even Major could pass her by without knowing it unless the wind happened to be right.

"We'll try up the road first," Jake decided. "Never can tell but what she might have gone there and got hit by some car."

They walked up the road toward Johnny's house and passed it. Allis must have gone to bed, for the place was dark. Reaching the hard-surfaced road, Johnny cast his light on it. The only tracks, already nearly filled by snow, had been made hours ago. Jake laid his finger alongside his nose and wrinkled his brow.

"I doubt if she'd come this far, but I'll give her a call." He whistled and called sharply, "Hi, Sally! Hiya!"

They turned back on the tracks they had made; if the hound had heard, she would come and follow them. Johnny knew that Jake was worried. Sally was his favorite hound, and as long as he wanted to hunt for her Johnny was willing to help him.

"Where do you want to look now?" he asked.

"We'll go back to the house. She might have come while we were away."

But only Jake's three chained hounds greeted them when they returned to the house. Jake stood at the door, pondering the best thing to do next. Inside, the three caged puppies heard them and wailed hungrily.

"She wouldn't get in trouble on the creek," Jake said finally. "The only thing I can think of is Ab Whitley's pasture. He's running a few cattle in the Cross Tangle Meadows and there's barbed wire there. Sally might have tangled in it."

As they waded the shallow creek, Jake's three horses, pawing snow to uncover grass, arched their necks and pranced skittishly away. The horses stopped just outside the beam of light and turned with raised heads to watch them curiously.

Johnny's light stabbed the darkness, probing the falling snow. The north wind blew softly against their cheeks and the sky was lighter. But it was a deceptive lightness that foretold more snow to come. It might be heavy, and if there was too much of it they would have difficulty getting into the heights tomorrow.

They broke out of the woods into an open meadow where Ab Whitley, a rancher from up the creek, ran a few head of cattle. Blinking his eyes against the wind, Johnny spotted a little knot of cows and calves with his light. Tails over their backs, they broke into a clumsy, careening run that took them out of the light beam. Jake studied them thoughtfully.

"There's somethin' been at those critters. They've been scared."

Just then a fierce growl bubbled in Major's throat and he strained forward on the chain. Jake and Johnny followed. Major swerved toward a bunch of spruces that grew near the creek, then stopped, bristling. Johnny swung his light in the direction the hound was facing.

At the edge of the evergreens, partly covered by snow, lay a dead bull and a dead hound.

# 4

# Devil Cat

Jake Kane stood transfixed, jaws clamped so tightly that little ridges stood out on either side of them. Johnny could feel the fury that gripped the older man at the loss of his favorite dog. When Jake finally spoke, his voice seemed to be gritting on sand.

"Your lion was here, Johnny. He got Sally." He said it as though he couldn't believe it. "Hold Major and let me have the light."

As Johnny took Major's chain he could feel the old hound shivering beside him. But the dog was tense rather than cold; Major knew there had been a lion about and was trembling in anticipation. Jake moved around, taking it very slowly in order to miss nothing. He went into the spruces, the light flashing like a ghost lamp through the green branches. Coming out, Jake moved a little way up into the meadow and cast about in a wide circle. Then he went back into the evergreens again. A few minutes later he came to Johnny's side. Though he was still seething inwardly, he spoke quietly.

"That cat is big; I haven't run across one his size in twenty years. He's cunnin' and mean and he knows people. Otherwise he wouldn't have come so close to you. But there's some things about him that still don't add up to the cats I know. The only reason I can think of for his growin' so big is because he's also smart, and if he's smart he knows you saw him. My guess is that he let himself be seen deliberately. Looks as though we've got a problem on our hands."

"How'd he come after the cattle?" Johnny asked.

"Through the spruces. They went in there to get out of the snow and there wasn't anythin' to it. He's a killer, too. There's three dead calves and a dead cow in there and he fed from only one of the calves. I've seldom known a lion to kill what he doesn't eat. This one just hit right and left. Probably the bull tried to defend what was left and that's why he got it."

"Should we get the hounds?" Johnny asked.

Jake shook his head. "Not tonight. With snow and darkness both against us the trail would be hard to follow, and that cat's ugly. He might tree and he might not, and if he don't he could get the rest of the pack. Meanwhile there's work to be done."

"What?"

"Those two calves and the cow haven't lain long enough to spoil; they'll be all right for eatin' and we'll butcher 'em for Ab. He won't want the lion-chewed calf or the bull, but they'll make dog feed."

While the night wore on they dressed out the slain cattle. When Johnny's hands seemed too cold to wield a knife any more, Jake built a small fire where they could warm themselves now and again. Then, with Sally's body cradled in his arms, Jake returned to his house and came back with two of his horses. Johnny and Jake tied ropes around the calves' necks, let the horses drag the carcasses over the soft snow to Jake's house, and there propped the belly cavities open to allow animal heat to escape. They needed both horses on the cow, but the bull and the mangled calf they could cut up and move easier because both were intended for dog feed.

When they were finished, Johnny's hands were numb and he felt too tired to move. Jake looked at him sympathetically.

"Come in and have a cup of coffee. It'll pick you up."

As they went into the house, the sleepy puppies, which Jake had fed during one of their trips in, merely stirred and yawned. Jake filled two thick cups with coffee from the pot on the back of the stove. Johnny saw by the clock that it was twenty minutes of two.

Jake said, "You're beat, Johnny. You sure you want to go out in the mornin'?"

"You bet!"

"Well, won't be any sense in startin' much before daylight; seven o'clock or thereabouts. Suppose you get here about quarter past six and have breakfast with me. I'll have it all ready."

Johnny stifled a yawn. "Okay with me."

"Tell Allis about the lion's raid, will you? Somebody'll be goin' by tomorrow and he can pass the word on to Ab. Ab can pick up the cow and calves in my yard; coyotes won't touch 'em there and the hounds are chained."

"I'll do that." Johnny finished his coffee. "Reckon I'll go home now and have some shut-eye."

"You'd better."

Rifle in hand, light at his belt, and Sounder plodding beside him, Johnny trudged homeward. When they got there, Sounder flopped wearily beside Pat. Johnny wrote a note to his grandfather, telling about the raid and the butchered cattle, then fell into bed himself.

The next morning, when Johnny returned to Jake's, the windows were squares of light against the morning blackness. His aches and weariness forgotten, Johnny sniffed eagerly at the welcome aroma of wood smoke. He went in and found Jake bent over the hot stove, a long-handled fork in his hand.

"I heard the dogs fussin' and knew you were on your way," Jake greeted Johnny. "Pour the coffee and we'll eat."

Jake heaped their plates with calves' liver, bacon, and fried potatoes. They ate in silence, and in quantity. There was a snow-filled wilderness ahead of them, and a long hunt, and it could be a long while before they ate again. Johnny buttered another slice of bread and with it sopped up the remnants on his plate. In their box, the three puppies mewed plaintively.

From the back of the stove Jake took a warming pot filled with remnants of the liver, crusts of bread, and an assortment of other foods that he had been saving. He emptied the pot into two tin dishes, then let the puppies out. All three went to one bowl, their long ears dangling in it as they ate. Buck seized a bone, left over from an earlier-made stew, and padded into a corner to chew it. When his two brothers approached hopefully, he warned them away with a puppyish growl. Johnny laughed.

"Looks as though he can take care of himself. What are they going to do while we're gone—have the run of the place?"

"Don't know that they can do any harm that hasn't already been done. Let's go."

They washed the dishes in Jake's wooden sink and stacked them in the cupboard. Then they went out into the lightening morning, where the hounds lay watching them expectantly. The dogs did not cry out, or tug impatiently at their chains, but they seemed tense and taut and Johnny knew that the hounds sensed they were going out to hunt this morning. Right now, Johnny thought, they acted almost like men waiting to go to work.

Jake said, "We'll catch ourselves a couple of horses first."

The horses were still on the other side of the creek, pawing snow to find grass, and they raised suspicious heads when they saw the men stirring. They weren't fond of work and hated to be caught, but Jake knew how to lure them.

He passed the snow-dusted carcasses of the cow and calves and went into the barn where they had hung the dog meat. When Johnny followed, Jake handed him a bridle. He took another himself, then lifted the hinged lid of a grain bin. Catching up a wooden scoop, he filled it half full of oats and went back outside, rattling the oats in the scoop as he did so. In a low voice he spoke to Johnny.

"When they stick their noses in, catch your horse. Don't take the blaze face. He's been lame."

"All right."

The horses looked at their master, stood uncertainly for a moment, then splashed across the unfrozen creek and with heads tossing came up to the barn. Eagerly, crowding each other, they thrust their noses into the grain scoop and began to lick up the oats. Johnny waited, and when Jake slipped his bridle reins around the neck of a tough little bay, Johnny did likewise. His horse pulled back, pretending to be startled, but Johnny slipped the bit in, buckled the throat latch, and tied his horse to a peg in the barn wall. Jake tied his mount beside Johnny's, and they saddled up. Then Jake loosed the hounds and for a moment sat in his saddle, thinking.

"We'll never pick his tracks up in the meadow," he said. "Snow's been blowing all night and they'll be covered. And that lion won't stay around here long; he might not be afraid of people but he's fed now and he'll lay up until he wants to feed again. We'll go up in the rimrock."

"Whereabouts?"

"The Sand Bluffs. That's the nearest place he'll find enough cover to suit him."

They rode their horses into the gravel highway, the hound pack at their heels. The dogs were tense and eager, and wanted to run, but Jake had taught his hounds to stay behind until he gave the word. Jake turned from the road up a narrow, rock-lined little canyon where straggling evergreens clung precariously to the rocks.

Far above was the plateau with its ponderosa pine, and in between was a tangle of rock, some of which was tumbled and scattered and some of which rose in almost sheer bluffs. This was part of the rimrock, endlessly tangled, ridged, and seamed. To one who did not know, it would have seemed inaccessible, but it was cut by paths and traverses that men and hounds could travel but horses could not. Johnny began to appreciate Jake's strategy.

The tangled rock maze above them furnished a hundred caves and fissures, in any one of which the lion could have comfortably lain up for a day. But the wind was blowing from the canyon straight up over the rim, sweeping snow before it as it drove into the ponderosa pine. Hounds on top of the rim should get the lion's scent. Then they would find his hiding place and after that the chase should not be too long. His stomach heavy with pirated veal, the lion would be in no mood to run very far before he treed.

"Far as we can go on horses," Jake announced. "We'll tie 'em here."

They stripped saddles and bridles from their horses, slipped halters on, and attached picket ropes. Then they tied the horses far enough apart so that they would not tangle each other's picket ropes and far enough from the surrounding brush so that they would not become snarled in that. Rifle in hand, Jake looked from the mass of rocks to the top of the rim.

"He's in there somewheres," he said, "lyin' up in a nice dry hole where he thinks nothin' can bother him. But he's goin' to be bothered, and right soon. Let's go up, Johnny."

"I'm with you."

They started climbing the slippery slope, while the hounds sniffed hopefully into the little winds that whispered about them. They were going hunting and they knew it. But Jake had not yet given the command to range out and hunt, and until he did the hounds would not know whether they were to take the trail of a lion, bobcat, bear, or whatever else Jake wanted.

With a sudden bass roar Rowdy left them and surged ahead. Jake's commanding voice summoned him back. Ears drooping, tail between his legs, Rowdy slunk back and walked ten feet in the rear. Jake looked at him sternly, and Rowdy's tail drooped a little more. Soon they reached an evergreen thicket, and found where a resting bobcat had bounced out, after attracting Rowdy's attention. The hounds looked inquiringly at Jake; the bobcat would be easy game.

"Stay!" Jake roared at them.

They ranged themselves about him, but all turned to face the enticing scent left by the bobcat. Jake stopped to catch his breath. Not yet breathless, but trying not to show it because Jake was, Johnny halted beside him.

"I thought it ruined hounds not to let them hunt, Jake?"

Jake nodded. "If I had a pack of young ones I'd send them off after the bobcat. But these are old dogs and I have to save them; let 'em roar off now and they won't have anythin' left when we jump the big one. Especially Major. He's good and he's smart. But he's gettin' old, like me."

They reached the rim and were struck squarely in the face by the wind that swept up it. A sudden scent assailed Johnny's nostrils and he identified it as the

odor of elk. If he could smell elk, the far more acute
noses of the hounds should certainly locate the lion in
the maze of rocks below them. Jake's strategy made
good sense.

But as they worked their way up the rim, Jake
looked more and more puzzled. They had come a
long way, and all the while the wind had been
blowing directly into the hounds' noses. But except
for the bobcat they had shown no sign of game that
they wanted to hunt. Pausing for breath again, Jake
looked at the tumbled rock below them.

"I can't figure it," he admitted. "He should have
been in there somewheres, but he's not. Where the
blazes did he go?"

"Do you suppose he stayed in the creek bottom?"
Johnny asked.

Jake shook his head. "Not that cat. The reason
there ain't as many lions as there used to be is
because they're hunted harder nowadays. Two-thirds
of the spring cubs are treed and killed every fall. It's
seldom nowadays you get a real old-timer. But that
one's no cub. From what I could see of his tracks I'd
judge he was four years old and maybe older. That
means he's been smart enough to run away from
hounds and too smart to hang out in the creek
bottoms. He's just out-foxed us."

They started back and were mounting a high rock
when Major halted and took a few steps at a direct
angle to their line of travel. Jake stopped, watching

the dog closely. He knew the senses of a good hound, and knew also that his dogs wouldn't strike off on their own unless there was good reason for it.

Major took a few more steps, and by now his pack mates were interested. Lacking Major's keen nose, as yet none of them had the scent. But they had followed him for so long that they knew he had one. Then, no longer in doubt, Major gave voice to a bellowing roar, straight into the teeth of the biting wind. He looked expectantly back.

"Take him, Major!" Jake urged. To Johnny he added, "That's lion."

"How do you know?"

"He'd tongue different for a bear or bobcat. We may have that old killer after all!"

Cautiously, following the delicate thread of scent, old Major went on into the wind. The other dogs followed unquestioningly, and disappeared in the swirling snow.

Jake stood still. He was sure that the dogs were on a lion and now he must decide approximately where the chase would take them. He listened intently to the tonguing pack leader as the hounds ran into the snow-dusted distance. The lion was north, in the pine country, and not down in any of the canyons or maze of rocks at all. Somewhere in the forest the running hounds would tree him, and before he decided on any course of action Jake wanted to know approximately where that would be. As he listened, the dogs seemed to swerve, so that they were running slightly northwest. All four hounds tongued steadily; they had found the track that Major had first smelled. A broad smile on his face, Jake turned to Johnny.

"We need our horses. I know just about where he'll tree."

"Do you think it's the one we want?"

"It must be. Come on."

With long, swinging strides they swung directly away from the pack and started downslope. Though the snowy footing on the rimrock was precarious for a man and impossible for a horse, there were a few passable trails. Jake knew almost where the hounds were going, and by cutting across country on trails that a horse could run, they'd get there much faster than they would by trying to follow the dogs on foot.

They burst through the screen of little evergreens where they'd left their horses and stopped short.

One horse lay on its back, both forelegs crookedly upthrust and its hind quarters twisted to one side. Snow partly covered a puddle of blood that had flowed from beneath the horse and congealed on the cold earth. A series of parallel gashes about which blood had frozen showed the work of a mountain lion.

Snow was churned and pounded where the other horse, in its frantic effort to escape, had reared and plunged until it finally broke its tether. Scuffed tracks in the snow showed where the horse had galloped down the narrow little canyon toward home.

Johnny suddenly felt cold, a little afraid, as though this were no beast but an evil, scheming enemy. While they were up in the rimrock with the hounds, the lion must have known all about them and what they were doing. From some high and lonely rock it might even have seen them come here and leave, and so knew that it was safe to slip down and attack the horses while they were away.

Gripping his rifle so tightly that his clenched knuckles showed white against the skin, Jake was casting about and examining tracks, his face a mask of fury.

"He was never up in the rimrock!" he said hoarsely. "He stayed in the canyon all along! That's why the hounds couldn't pick him up; we were too far away."

"What about the lion they're on?" Johnny asked.

"Must be a different one. Johnny, I'll nail this cat's hide to my barn door if it takes all winter! Look at this track!"

Johnny went over to examine one of the lion's tracks, clearly imprinted in the snow. He felt the hair on the back of his neck bristle. The track was huge, and there was so little snow in it that every toe was very clear. Wider than the span of Johnny's hand, the track could have been left only by a monstrous lion.

"Let's go after him!" he said eagerly.

Jake shook his head. "Men can't run a lion down. We need hounds. Wish they were here!"

"What do we do now?"

"Go get 'em."

They made their way through fluffy snow up a canyon, and climbed a side draw to swing back to the top. It was hard work. The bitter wind made them look down instead of straight ahead. Snow reached to the calves of their legs, and in drifted places, to their thighs. They might have followed the path they had broken coming down, but Jake was taking the shortest way, directly toward where he thought the dogs might be.

They reached the top, rested again, and Jake let his jaw hang slack while he listened. There was no sound save that made by the wind. An hour had elapsed before they finally heard Major's tree bark. They turned toward the sound, and after twenty minutes stopped again.

Both heard the hounds clearly now; they had treed their lion and were tonguing it. Johnny identified each of the four dogs by their different voices as he and Jake made their way toward them.

There was a moment's lull in the storm and Major's voice rang like a bell through the short silence. Having the exact direction now, they veered to the left. Jake knew the patch of trees in which the lion had gone up and almost the exact tree in which they would find it. A hundred times or more his hounds had gone racing through this part of the rimrock, and with certain exceptions, such as the big lion they'd hoped to get, most lions acted pretty much alike. They had their favorite runs, their favorite haunts, and most of them, brought to bay in this area, would either climb the same tree or go up one very near it.

Through the swirling snowflakes, they saw the hounds. The lion had treed in a small pine against which another tree had fallen. Seeking a hold with his stubby nails, Major was halfway up the leaning tree, and the fact that the snow was brushed off ahead of him was proof that he had climbed farther before and fallen off. Even as they watched he started up again, scraping for a hold on the round, snow-slippery trunk. He plunged from it into the snow beneath the tree and got up limping.

A tawny-brown patch of fur, the lion was plastered so tightly to the tree's trunk that at first it seemed to be part of it. But its head was up, its ears alert, as it both watched and listened to the eager hounds. So intent was it on the dogs that it never saw the hunters, and save for a single explosive moment, it never felt the soft-nosed bullet that smashed through its brain.

The lion tumbled out of the tree, a soft and formless mass that landed limply in the snow. The hounds rushed in, but when the lion did not move they merely sniffed disinterestedly at it and sat on their haunches looking expectantly at Jake. Old Major got up to circle around the pack, and when he did he held his right hind leg clear of the snow. Jake leaned his rifle against a tree and dropped to his knees to examine the injured leg. When he looked up at Johnny, his face was grim.

"This is that big lion's lucky day."

"Is Major hurt much?"

"No, but he can't run for a while and I won't send the other three against a lion like that without him. They'd get in trouble sure."

Expertly Jake scalped the lion, running his knife around its ears and the top of its head and lifting that part off. Lion skins were worth little except in tourist season, but there was a forty-dollar bounty on every lion killed. However, all one had to present in order to collect the bounty were the ears and scalp.

"I'll come back with a horse and pick up the saddles," Jake said. "Easiest way for us now is right down the bluff and onto the road."

They started through the pines toward a canyon that led to the road. The four hounds trailed wearily behind them. Jake was grim and silent, and Johnny knew what he was thinking.

But though he hunted all winter long, Jake did not nail the big lion's hide to his barn door.

## 5

# Kane Hound

Though snow still lingered on the peaks, and would be there long after summer heat came to the valleys and canyons, spring was well under way in the lower country. Green leaves had already uncurled on the aspens and even the oaks were in bud. The tumbling little streams were entirely free of ice. Only on an occasional cold night would a light frost whiten the roofs and make brittle the dead grasses in exposed meadows. Winter was past and would not return for a long while.

It was Saturday, and Johnny Torrington awakened early to a delicious sense of anticipation. Jake Kane had introduced his three hound pups to the pack, he was going to take them on their first hunt, and he had invited Johnny to go along.

As usual, for a few minutes Johnny remained in bed, savoring the warmth of his blankets. Even when summer was at its height, and the sun burned hotly during the noon hours, the nights in this high country were always cool. When Johnny got out of bed he scrambled hastily into his clothes, drew heavy leather shoes over his stockinged feet, and slipped on a light wool jacket.

Once outside, he buttoned the jacket, for though there had been no frost, the temperature was not far above the freezing mark. Johnny struck briskly down the road, wondering hungrily what Jake would have for breakfast.

This outdoor life he loved, and more than once he had felt regret because he had been born into an age whose trend was more and more toward mechanized and sheltered living. Often it seemed to Johnny that the old days Jake and Allis described must have been very good ones. After hearing their stories of great hounds and fierce game, he wanted to become a hunter himself. But the day of commercial hunters was passing, and he had to prepare himself for the problems presented by a modern world. That was why he had chosen forestry for a career, with its emphasis on outdoor life.

However, there would always be hunting and hounds to do it. He thought of Buck, the red pup. Both Allis and Jake had declared that he had the makings of a truly great hound, and Johnny knew that Jake had refused to sell him though he had had several opportunities to do so. Johnny respected his grandfather's and Jake's opinions, but he didn't see how anybody could really know what a good hunting hound would do until it actually hunted. As he walked along he was struck by the fact that Buck was the only dog he'd ever seen with which he had not been able to make friends. Not that the red pup had ever displayed any viciousness toward Johnny. It was more that Buck was strictly a one-man dog who had already found his man in Jake Kane. Other people were simply tolerated.

Daylight glowed in a cloudless sky, but yet there was no hint of sun when Johnny came to Jake's house. The four older dogs greeted him, and the two bluetick pups frisked about almost hysterically. Only Buck remained in the shadows and did not rise. For a moment Johnny played with the hound pack, trying to give each its due share of petting and no more. Then he went into the house.

"Morning, Jake." Johnny sniffed hungrily at the contents of the two skillets sputtering on the stove. "Smells good."

"It'll stick by you," Jake assured him. "Mutton chops and fried potatoes."

Johnny nodded. He knew where the mutton came from.

Each spring thousands of sheep followed the receding winter into the heights, and were preyed upon by lions, coyotes, foxes, and bobcats. The sheep men paid Jake for scalps he could show of any of these predators and in addition kept him supplied with as much mutton as he wanted.

Outside there sounded a sudden fierce snarl followed by a shrill yelp and a soft whimpering. Jake grinned.

"Pups on their first job, like youngsters, sure get their hair rubbed the wrong way now and again."

Johnny knew what Jake meant. When the puppies were very young, they had been regarded by the older dogs in much the same light that adults look upon young children. Most of the time they had great leeway, and their only punishment was an occasional light nip that hurt their feelings but nothing else. But now the pups were being integrated into the pack. They were expected to become a working portion of it and to shoulder their share of the work. The older hounds understood that puppyish antics were not a part of pack life, and the pups were learning the fact the hard way.

Johnny helped Jake put the food on the table, and filled thick mugs with strong coffee. As they sat down, Johnny asked a leading question, hoping to draw Jake out.

"Are we going after lion?"

"Not with three pups on their first hunt. I want to see them in action against somethin' else before I ask them to do any lion huntin'. We'll go up Calliver Canyon. There's a lot of rabbits up there. What's more, Bud Caudell sent a flock of his sheep up Calliver a couple of days ago. Bobcats will be hangin' around the sheep and we should have no trouble jumpin' one."

"I hope so," Johnny said eagerly. "You'll have a big pack again, now that you're adding the three pups."

Jake shook his head. "I'm keepin' it at four, or at the most five if all the pups turn out all right. Five dogs are all I can afford to feed, so I'm sellin' Rowdy and Flutter."

Johnny nodded. Rowdy and Flutter were two of Jake's lesser dogs. Rowdy, named because he was just that, and Flutter, a trim little female who always skittered about before she got any trail straight, had never been leaders on any hunt. But they were Kane hounds, where the least were good and the best were marvelous. Selling them would leave Jake with Major, Doe, and at least two of the pups. If they all turned out very well, maybe he would keep all three. Either way he would have a very good pack.

Daylight was full-blown, and the sun was lightening the sky behind the eastern mountains by the time they had washed the dishes and gone outside. The hounds crowded anxiously about them, wagging their tails and blowing through flabby lips. But except for a brief glance at Johnny, Buck had eyes only for Jake.

Johnny looked at the red pup appraisingly. All winter long, with his two brothers, Buck had slept in the box beside Jake's stove. He had grown big and strong there, so that now he was a powerful dog with a frame almost full grown but with the looseness of puppyhood evident in his every line and motion. He

seemed definitely more mature than his two brothers.

The four older hounds fell sedately in behind their
master and Johnny. The red pup walked with them,
as though he knew and could keep his place. But the
two young blueticks ranged ahead or at either side,
snapping at flies, pouncing on wind-ruffled leaves,
and otherwise acting like puppies. Johnny turned to
look again at Buck. The pup did not return his look.
Walking just far enough from Jake so that there was
no danger of his being kicked in the jaw by a
backward-swinging heel, he seemed to be making
almost a conscious effort to align himself with the
older dogs.

When they came to the creek, the hounds waded
the icy water, while Jake and Johnny, crossed on a
narrow plank bridge. In the meadow beyond, Jake's
two horses arched friendly necks and snorted softly
through their noses. Johnny turned to the old hunter.

"You never did get the big lion that killed your
horse, did you?"

"I never even saw his track again," Jake said sadly.
"But I think he's seen me. Lots of times when I
walked up on the rim I had the idea that I was bein'
watched. But I never found anythin' and the dogs
never picked up anythin'. One of these days, though,
that lion will be heard from."

"How do you know?"

"He's a devil cat," Jake said shortly. "Did you ever
think who'd be boss of this region if lions had men's

brains? Lucky they haven't, or we'd be layin' out on the rimrock while lions hunted us. Few lions are dumb, but every now and again an extra-smart one comes along and that big lion's it. He hasn't raided around here since the night he killed my Sally and Ab's cattle. But it's just because he hasn't felt like leavin' the rimrock. He will, and we'll all be hearin' from him."

"How do you know he hasn't just left this part of the country?"

"Johnny, time you've hunted lions as long as I have, you know some things about 'em that you can't put into words. I know that lion is here because I know it."

Johnny said no more. They were climbing now, going into the rocky country around Calliver Canyon. In this sort of travel a man was as fast as a horse and there was no danger of risking a valuable mount. Jake stopped to get his breath and Johnny pulled up too. He wasn't winded at all, but he knew Jake was and didn't want to embarrass him by keeping on.

Far across the canyon, on a grassy slope, Bud Caudell's sheep looked like so many gray boulders. Johnny saw a sheep dog, made small by distance, rush out and herd some stragglers back into the flock. Johnny nodded, appreciating Jake's reasoning about the chances of jumping a bobcat.

Sheep dogs were more than just good; in their devotion to and understanding of their job they were little short of miraculous. But two or three sheep dogs could not watch every member of a big flock like this all the time and predators were bound to take their toll. Bobcats with designs on the flock were undoubtedly lying up right now, waiting for darkness. The dogs should strike a track soon, and a fresh one.

Except for Buck, who trailed steadfastly at Jake's heels, the hounds had been ranging here and there and sniffing at various piles of rocks and bushes. Once the two bluetick puppies yapped hysterically after a rabbit that bounced away from them. When they panted back, Jake worked them over with a switch. The chastened puppies, tails between their legs, slunk sheepishly to the rear. They were on their way to learning that a dog that would chase rabbits was not of the quality Jake wanted.

Johnny walked on beside Jake, until suddenly both were halted by a shrill, excited yelp from Buck. They turned around.

No longer directly behind Jake's heels, the red puppy had halted perhaps fifty feet away. His head turned sideways, into the wind, and he was taut as a stretched rubber band. Slowly, as though walking on something that he feared would break, he left the line of march and stalked toward a thicket. His head was up, ears dangling, nostrils twitching. The red puppy had an elusive thread of scent and he was following it for all he was worth.

The two bluetick puppies merely stared without comprehending, but the older dogs trotted back. Major raised his head, roared, and took over. Side by side, Major and the red puppy went into the thicket. A moment later Major's steady trail bark mingled with the puppy's squeal. Then the pack was away, the two bluetick puppies straining to catch up.

"I knew he had the heart," Jake said proudly. "Now I know he has the nose too. Major missed that one."

"I guess most hounds would have missed it," Johnny said.

"Not Sally. She would have got it. I think that red pup's got Sally's nose."

One of the bluetick puppies straggled back, tongue dangling from open jaws, and Jake looked at it without speaking. But Johnny knew what he was thinking. The puppy probably would be a passable hunter, but no dog that turned back could run with Jake's hounds.

The bluetick trailed at their heels as they set off to follow the pack.

When the red pup first caught the elusive scent, he had followed its source instinctively. Then the older dogs joined him, and Buck tried to crowd in ahead. Major nipped him savagely. Not subdued at all, but respectful, Buck followed. The scent strengthened as they drew closer to it, and in his eagerness the red pup overran, then stopped. The four older hounds went tonguing into the wilderness.

The red puppy strained after them because that seemed the right thing to do. His heart pounded and his blood ran fast as he strove to catch up. He could not, for the older dogs had a head start. Buck clung determinedly to the trail, his nostrils filled with cat scent. He heard the four dogs change from their trail bark to the tree bark.

When Buck finally caught up, the four hounds were baying around a fallen tree upon which stood a snarling bobcat. He was big, thirty pounds or heavier, and he was very angry. He slashed with his paws as Major feinted, then whirled to meet Doe, who came in from the other side. They were joined by the bluetick pup that had not turned back.

Suddenly, the bobcat leaped. There was a mingled shriek and snarl from the bluetick pup that the cat pinned to earth. Fortunately for the bluetick, Major sprang again, Doe closed from the other side, and Rowdy and Flutter came charging in. They surged over the fighting cat, and the red pup flung himself into the fight with them. He felt a raking claw gash his ribs and he did not care. His jaws sought the weakening cat, and he ground them hard.

He was a hunting dog now.

## 6

# The Hunter

The day Jake and Johnny had gone hunting the big lion in the rimrock, Jake had guessed wrong. An ordinary lion would have gone to the maze of rocks—the nearest hiding place—and the hounds would have scented him there. But, as Jake suspected, this was no ordinary lion.

While fierce winds blew about him and covered his tracks, he had gone up the opposite side of the canyon, lain up in a copse of spruces, and watched Jake and Johnny. When they had tied their horses, and climbed out of sight with the hounds, the lion stalked and killed the horse out of sheer nervous fury. Then he traveled fast, listening for baying hounds, and when they did not come he slowed his pace. Night was approaching, and experience had taught the lion that night was a safe time. He killed a deer, fed, and lay up in a thicket.

For a week he wandered, following the deer but

always going deeper into the wilderness so that, at the end of a week, he was in a vast and lonely area of mingled pine and rock country which few men saw even in summer and almost nobody visited in winter. Deer that had come down from the heights offered easy hunting. It was good living, all winter long.

Then, with spring, the deer scattered back into their high pastures and the lion followed. Gone was winter's simple living, but because the lion was a good hunter, he fared well.

One day, from the shelter of a copse high on a mountain, he saw his first big flock of sheep, just moved to the high upland pastures for summer grazing. While the sun shone, he stayed in the copse, watching. As soon as the first long shadows of evening fell across the peaks, he began his attack.

The lion slunk cautiously, keeping the wind in his nose so that he could smell everything without being scented himself. The oily odor of sheep was very heavy, but through it the lion located exactly the two dogs that were with the flock. He also scented the remnants of the herder's fire, and the herder himself, in his tent.

When the lion attacked, he was lightning fast. Springing forward, he struck down two sheep while the rest scattered before him. Terrified bleating filled the night as the lion leaped erratically to the left or right to follow and pull more sheep down. He heard the dogs yelping and when he felt one of them snapping at his heels he whirled to slap with his paw. After a single, choked scream that broke in the middle, the dog was still.

The lion's ears were laid back, his face a snarling mask, as he slaughtered sheep madly. Killing lust surged within him, and fury overwhelmed reason, so that when he saw a man rushing at him with a knife in his hand, the lion did not hesitate at all. He sprang, striking as he did so, and the man went down beneath his rush.

Then, while the single remaining dog yapped ineffectively at his heels, he fled into the night.

It was late afternoon when Bud Caudell steered his pickup truck into Jake Kane's yard. Major, Doe, Buck, and the bluetick puppy that Jake had kept, barked a perfunctory challenge, then lay down again as Jake came out of the house.

For a moment the lean sheepman regarded the four hounds moodily, then turned to Jake.

"Cut your pack down, haven't you?"

"Some," Jake admitted. "But these four are as many as I can feed. What's on your mind?"

Bud gestured toward the hounds. "You're going to need a new lead dog. Major's no pup."

"I'll have one in that red pup soon's he gets a little more experience," Jake said. "Did you come to talk dog or what?"

"Do you know Esteban Oregay?"

"Isn't he one of your herders?"

"Not just one of them. He's the best I ever saw, but something's happened to him."

"Come on in," Jake said pointedly. While Jake poured coffee from the always-ready pot, Bud Caudell dropped into a chair and drummed nervously on the table.

"I took supplies out to Esteban this morning," he went on. "He had his flock in the meadow below Crown Castle."

"So?"

"So I found Esteban with one dog left and just about able to stagger himself. A lion got into his sheep and then hit him."

Jake looked sharply at his visitor, remembering the lion that had followed Johnny Torrington, remembering a winter's night, with dead cattle and a dead hound, remembering a horse dead in the canyon spruces. All winter long nobody had seen the big lion nor had he raided again. But Jake had known that he would come again and now he had.

"Was it a big lion?" Jake asked quietly.

"From the tracks I found it's the biggest one that's been in these parts in twenty years. Forty-nine sheep he got, and Esteban, and a dog."

"How is Esteban?"

"He sure is stove up. A broken right arm and four cracked ribs plus enough gashes and scratches to do any normal man for a lifetime. It would have killed anybody except a Basque herder. We took him to the hospital, and they say he'll pull through all right."

"Good. So you want me to get the lion?"

"Somebody has to get him," Bud Caudell exploded. "Allis Torrington's too old. That leaves you. Naturally I don't like to lose sheep, and I hate even worse to see one of my herders lion-beat. Especially Esteban. But that's not all. This isn't a normal cat."

"What do you mean?"

Bud Caudell shrugged. "Ever hear of a lion knocking down a flock of sheep and then tackling the herder too? That cat's crazy, and if he did it once he'll do it again."

"Yes, he'll hit again," Jake agreed.

Caudell looked keenly at him. "What do you know about him?"

"Plenty. Last winter he killed some of Ab Whitley's cattle, my Sally dog, and one of my horses while Johnny Torrington and I were huntin' him in the rimrock. My hounds have been on his trail and I agree with you that he ain't normal."

"What do you make of him?"

"I can't make any sense at all out of what he's been doin'. He don't act like any lion I've ever run across."

"But you'll get him?"

"I'll hunt him."

"All right, Jake. We'll leave it at that. I'm going to see Joe Martin, Tom Shuderm, and Ole Swenson. They have sheep in the high pastures too, and they can't afford to take chances with them. If you'll keep on this lion's tail and give up all other hunting, the four of us will underwrite your expenses. Go to Connelly's store for whatever you need; I'll tell Connelly you're coming. The day you bring that lion in there'll be five hundred dollars for you. Fair enough?"

"Fair enough. I'll see you when I have somethin' to report."

Bud Caudell left and Jake stood tapping his knuckles on the table. The lion had struck again, as he had known it would. It would come a third time, and a fourth, and keep on coming until somebody stopped it. There was something out of the ordinary about this lion, something fiendish . . .

Jake shook his head irritably. The lion was big, it was clever, and it knew as much about men as they knew about lions. But it was no super beast. It would leave tracks, and Jake knew that his hounds could find anything that left a scent. On sudden impulse he went outside.

The hounds came eagerly to see what he might have for them, and Jake scratched their ears. The bluetick puppy sat down in the dust to dig his right ribs with his right hind paw. When Jake offered them no morsel of food Major and Doe wandered back to sprawl in their beds. But Buck sat down in front of Jake and pushed his cold muzzle into Jake's hand. His eyes were soft, and glowing with love. Jake tickled the pup, and looked at him fondly.

There are always superior creatures among any group of animals, the leaders of their kind, and Jake knew that Buck was such a one. It was not size that made him so, for he was no bigger than any Kane hound. Nor was it necessarily physical perfection. Rather, it was something that lay deep inside, some extra quality of heart or brain. Buck had now proven his worth on a number of bobcats and had been in on the killing of two lions. He had a wonderful nose, all the courage of a fighting cock, and an instinctive knowledge of what was right in any given situation.

"You're goin' to be a hound," Jake murmured. "A hound like I've seldom had before. If Major was a few years younger, or you had another season's experience, we'd have that hellion's hide inside a week."

But the pup lacked experience, the indispensable ingredient that must mold and polish even the greatest courage, ability, and intelligence. Major and Doe would have to lead the hunt. He thought sadly of Sally as he went back into the house. Still, it was a lion he must hunt, and nothing more. Jake oiled his rifle, laid out his hunting togs, a knife and hatchet, and wrapped a small packet of food. Then he hesitated.

As age went, he was not old. But he had followed many a hound pack, sat before many a campfire, and only he knew how lonely they were becoming. It was strange because he had not always felt that way, but he did now. He thought of Johnny Torrington, and looked at his calendar. School was out, and maybe Johnny would go with him.

Ordering the hounds back, Jake walked up the road to Allis's house, where he found the old man at the kitchen table, mixing dough.

"Watch what you're doing!" Allis bellowed. "Just because you live like a pig is no sign everybody else should too!"

Jake grinned and moved away from the table. "Sorry to disturb your bakin'. Johnny here?"

"Would he be here when he's got work to do?"

"Oh. Is Johnny workin'?"

"Didn't I say he was? He went to work for Ab Whitley, digging a ditch so Ab can have water piped right into his house. I don't know what's coming over folks nowadays; I've never had running water. Don't want it, either. A body should do some things for himself. But Ab's paying Johnny a dollar a day and when he's done he gets three calves. Going to raise 'em, Johnny is, to help pay his way through forestry school." Allis looked meaningly at Jake. "If you'd have done that when you were Johnny's age, you wouldn't be a useless old coot of a lion hunter now."

Jake chuckled. "Like you, eh, Allis? Tell Johnny I've gone off on a hunt, will you?"

"I'll tell him," Allis grunted.

The four hounds trailing behind his horse, Jake left the next morning, two hours before dawn. Crown Castle was a sheer bluff, a great monument of rock that dominated green meadows, and it was a long way back in the wilderness. But horses could get there and Jake knew all the trails. He swerved from the main road, splashed across a creek that the hounds had to swim, and started up a rock-ribbed canyon whose walls were dotted with little clumps of pine and dwarf cedar.

Buck whined anxiously in the pre-dawn darkness, and ran a little way to one side. Jake heard Major's deep snuffling, and for a moment he was indecisive. Some animal that the hounds wanted to hunt had crossed or been close to here, and for a moment he was tempted to let the dogs run it. But at the best it was a wild chance that it would be the lion he wanted, and if the chase should be a long one he might be sidetracked all day. Jake spoke softly to the hounds and ordered them on.

Daylight found him far up the canyon, amidst swirling mist that rose from the rill he had been following. A bull elk, its head topped by grotesque clubs of velvet-colored antlers, left the pool where it had been drinking and loped out of sight. Jake watched it admiringly. The bull was fully as big as a horse, and there was not much cover to conceal it. But the elk needed only seconds to fade into it and disappear.

Jake mounted a slope at the head of the canyon, came to a wide meadow, and found what was left of this herd of Bud Caudell's sheep.

They were not grazing in a compact bunch, but were scattered across the meadow. Two sheep dogs stood where they could watch the flock to best advantage. Jake noticed a water hole rimmed with brown mud, and beaten trails leading down to it. At one side of the meadow, under a single big pine that looked strangely out of place in the open grassland, the herder's tent was pitched. Thin blue smoke from a campfire drifted up through the pine branches.

Jake looked around to make sure his dogs were at heel. They weren't interested in sheep, but if any of the four drifted too close to the flock the sheep dogs might misinterpret their intentions and start a battle. Finding his dogs close by, Jake put his horse at a slow walk toward the tent until he recognized who was replacing Esteban Oregay.

The herder was Sammy Wilson, a stone-faced man who had drifted into the country about ten years ago. Nobody knew where he had come from and nobody asked. Sammy knew a little about everything, and not much about anything, and until he had gone to work for Bud Caudell he had found odd jobs wherever he could.

He didn't know much about herding sheep, but he knew enough to get by and Jake suspected that he was here partly because he was the only man Bud had to send. Jake also suspected that Sammy was here because nothing frightened him, although Jake had never decided whether he was a man of iron nerve or whether he just did not recognize danger when it threatened. Two years ago Sammy had been shaving himself in a bunkhouse when it caught fire, but he had refused to leave until he had finished shaving. Sammy's other distinguishing characteristic was a strong disinclination to any kind of conversation.

"Mornin'!" Jake called cheerfully. "Nice day."

"Yeah."

"Lost any more sheep to cats?"

"Nope."

"Has there been any sign of that big lion?"

"Nope."

"You're gettin' along all right, huh?"

"Yeah."

With the toe of his shoe Sammy nudged the coffeepot toward the fire. He laid mutton chops in a skillet, pushed a tin of biscuits up to warm, and jerked a thumb toward the fire. Jake licked his lips. He'd eaten before he left home, but brisk air and riding had made him hungry again. He rein-haltered his horse, ordered the hounds to lie on the grass beside him, and waited for the meal to cook.

While he waited, Jake let his eyes stray over the grazing flock and tried in his mind to determine a proper course of action. There was nothing he could do right here, for the raid had obviously taken place elsewhere. After the lion's attack, the sheep would have been moved from their former pasture; the carcasses of the dead sheep would have befouled that.

"Did Oregay move the sheep?" Jake asked.

"Nope."

"Did you?"

"Yeah."

"Where were they before?"

Sammy pointed. "Two miles." With this burst of information he served up the chops and poured coffee.

Jake ate gravely. "Well, thanks for the breakfast, Sammy. Only thing is, I hate all this chin-choppin' with my meals. You sure are a talkative cuss. If Bud Caudell comes, tell him I was here."

"Okay."

Jake mounted his horse and rode on. The scene of the raid was farther up the canyon and Jake wanted to see for himself what had taken place there. It was a long chance, a very long one, that he might pick up the lion's tracks. He doubted if the killer had lingered near the scene of his crime. Any tracks would be very old.

Jake saw Crown Castle, a long shaft of red rock surmounted by what, if enough imagination were used, might have been a crown. The hounds tagged behind the horse, seemingly interested in nothing. As Jake rose in his stirrups to scan the meadows, a black buzzard rose gracefully into the sky and winged away. Jake swerved toward the spot, and as he came near a dozen more buzzards got up, then a gray coyote streaked across the meadow. Jake reached instinctively toward his rifle, but the coyote was far out of range and running.

The slain sheep lay here and there, at odd-spaced intervals where the lion had overtaken them. Jake went from one to another, reading what had happened by the position of the carcasses. Coming on the flock, the lion had raced along with the sheep and stampeded them. He had apparently struck with machine-like efficiency, so that every blow meant another dead sheep.

Jake came to the place where Esteban Oregay had pitched his tent, and noticed that the last carcass lay within ten feet of it. The sign was easy to read here. Stampeding toward the tent, the sheep had awakened Esteban and brought him out, knife in hand. The lion must have worked with lightning speed. Certainly, if Esteban had not heard him when the carnage began, he had known very shortly thereafter. He must have rushed out of his tent as soon as possible, but still the lion had been able to strike down many more before the herder arrived. It had been blind, senseless carnage. Coming face to face with Esteban, the lion had unhesitantly leaped at the man. But he was not completely without fear of man. Having struck Esteban, his nerve had failed him and he had fled.

Jake dismounted and let his dangling hand brush the red pup's head.

"He ran after he hit Esteban," Jake said to Buck, "and all he's got to run in is a few million acres of the most busted-up country in North America. What are we goin' to do about it now?"

Buck wagged his tail and shoved his moist nose deeper into Jake's cupped hand. Jake rein-haltered his horse and turned back to count the dead sheep. As Bud Caudell had told him, there were forty-nine. Buzzards and coyotes had been tearing at them, but there was no indication that the lion had eaten any. Jake narrowed his eyes. The lion had not raided because he was hungry, but because he wanted to slaughter.

Jake looked at the folded line of peaks and bluffs that rose in the distance. They were an endless array; sheer cliffs, walled canyons, tangled windfalls. The lion might be anywhere, and guessing where he was was tantamount to guessing which cow in a herd would switch its tail to the left first. At the very least it would be a long, hard hunt, complicated by the fact that this lion was so very cunning.

Buck was sniffing at the grass in which the dead sheep lay, working his nostrils and blowing audibly through his cheeks. Some faint lion scent was apparently still clinging, and the pup was getting it even though the sheep cast a powerful stench. The red pup ran a little way and Jake watched hopefully. But after a few minutes Buck halted, baffled. Undaunted, he came back for another unsuccessful try.

Clear in Jake's mind was a picture of the lion track as he had seen it. He would recognize this one should he run across it again if only because of its size. But first he had to find it. Jake mounted his horse and rode slowly across the meadow.

The bluetick puppy broke, and went yelling wildly off. Angrily Jake called him back to heel, but rode in the direction that the pup had bolted. The dogs were tense and alert, straining eagerly, but they would not break again without command. Jake got off his horse and walked toward a thumb of trees that reached down and crooked into the meadow. A spring welled up in the trees, and a thin watercourse trickled down to form a reed-bordered pool in the meadow.

Carefully Jake inspected the soft ground on either side of the watercourse, and found where a big bobcat had walked there lately. It must have been what the bluetick puppy had scented. For a moment Jake debated whether to let his hounds run the bobcat, and decided against it. The dogs wanted to hunt and were spoiling for a run, but Jake still hoped to find the big lion's tracks and if he did he wanted to start the hounds on it as fresh as possible.

He rode out of the meadow and into the surrounding pines. They were on a hogbacked ridge, a gently sloping belt of trees that began in one rough section of rimrock, almost trailed out in another, then joined up with the great forest of ponderosa pine. The ridge should be a favorite passageway for lions and bobcats that wanted to get from one part of the rimrock to another. Elk that pastured in the meadow by night might come to the ridge in order to have shelter by day, but there would be few deer. They preferred places that their enemies, the lions, did not travel quite so regularly.

Again the bluetick puppy broke and again, angrily, Jake summoned him back to heel. He dismounted and found the tracks of four lions, obviously a female with three cubs. For a moment he stood uncertainly. If he ordered the dogs to hunt, the least they would probably do was tree the three cubs and it was a tempting prospect. But Jake went on.

The big lion would be a real prize, and bagging it would certainly win the sheepmen's undying gratitude. But for Jake something greater was involved. The lion presented a challenge such as he had never before known. He had a curious feeling which he could not help that the lion was superior to a human, although in his mind he knew that no such thing could be. If he bagged the big cat, he would prove that to himself.

Jake came to the narrowest part of the hogback and looked down both sides on a wild and weird tangle. Vari-colored rocks, spotted here and there with clusters of green trees, stretched as far as the eye could see. It was a wild and wonderful spectacle, rock country such as few people ever saw. For color and sheer beauty it was unmatched, but Jake knew the awful obstacles in the path of anyone who tried to hunt it or even travel it.

The spires and monuments, that looked so smooth from a distance, were laced with ledges, seamed with fissures, and honeycombed with caves. To the incautious or ignorant it could be a dangerous country. Some of the canyons had gentle slopes, but one might be traveling along and suddenly find himself on the rim of a precipice. In places the rock might crumble beneath one's feet. Loose shale was apt to slide.

He knew that was where the lion had gone.

Buck found scent on the far side of the rimrock, and went straight toward it. Jake rein-haltered his horse, called the red pup back, and kept the dogs at heel while he went to the place Buck indicated. He murmured under his breath.

The big lion had not traveled the ridge at all, but after slaughtering the sheep must have gone directly into the wild rock country to the north. Here on this narrow portion of the ridge he had climbed out of the north side to go down into the south. Jake found where he had scraped in the loose shale—scratched with either hind foot to heap a little mound of dirt— and defiled it. Scent lingered more strongly on the scrape, which explained why the red pup had found it.

The hounds sat down, quivering and anxious to run, while Jake examined the scrape carefully and whistled at the size of the track beside it. He stood back.

"All right, Buck. See what you can do. You have the best nose."

Major and Doe and the bluetick, while anxious to take part, remained in their places when Buck went forward. The red hound sniffed at the scrape, then ran a little way down the hill to verify some scent that had come from there. Snuffling audibly, he came back to examine the scrape again. A step at a time, he crossed the ridge and went a little way down the opposite slope. He came back to try again, and a third time. Each time he faltered; the track was too old. Jake called him to heel, mounted, and rode two hundred yards up the hogback.

He dismounted, leading his horse down a rocky little trail that was never more than two yards from the rim of a sheer rock wall and sometimes literally overhung it. This was no place to ride; should the horse fall he would take his rider with him. Safe at last on the floor of a canyon, Jake mounted and rode again.

At least, he thought with grim humor, he had narrowed the search down. Considering the situation, that was not a vast amount of help because there was still a few million acres of rimrock here on the south side. It was going to be next to impossible to find the lion in it and he needed a good, hot trail, one his hounds could follow. But he could not hope to find that trail unless he went to look for it. Certainly the lion was not going to advertise his presence.

All afternoon Jake traveled the canyons and breaks, and twice more the hounds discovered bobcat scent. But Jake did not want bobcats, and he was handicapped by the horse. It was impossible to search all the places he would have liked to see because the horse could not get into some of them. Nor did Jake dare leave it alone. He had no wish to come back and find another horse dead.

That night, while his hounds sprawled about him, Jake slept in a rock-bound canyon beside a tumbling stream. There had not been another sign of the lion.

# 7

# The Hunted

All through the rest of the school year Johnny Torrington had worked hard in an effort to bring his grades up. As a result, he had ended the year well within the upper third of his class. He had applied for a scholarship, but was far too much the realist to count on it. There were four scholarships for Johnny's school, a hundred and fifteen students competing for them, and he was sure that his grades weren't high enough. Allis didn't have money to send Johnny on to college. Facing the situation squarely, Johnny knew that it was up to him to get his coveted degree in forestry engineering. So when Ab Whitley had offered Johnny a job at the end of the school year, he was quick to accept it.

He might have taken prevailing wages, but when Ab offered him his choice of that or a dollar a day and three calves from Ab's dairy herd, Johnny saw the advantages in the latter offer. Allis owned twenty acres of fenced but unused pasture land. It would cost nothing to keep the calves while summer lasted, and when winter forced their being brought inside, they would need only grain and hay. The hay Johnny could cut on Allis's land. The grain he would buy with the dollar a day Ab was paying in addition to the calves. Eventually he'd get twice as much as he would with straight wages.

The source of Ab's projected water supply was a never-failing, never-freezing spring high on the side of one of the red bluffs. No watercourse trickled down from it for the spring had its own subterranean outlets, but not in the memory of the oldest settler had the bubbling water failed. Ab planned to pipe the water directly from the spring down to his house. That meant burying the pipe below the frost line.

With pick and shovel, Johnny began the ditch for the pipe a few feet from the lip of the spring. As he loosened the red dirt with his pick and cast it to one side with his shovel, he thought of how much more fun it would be if he were lion or bobcat hunting in the mountains with Jake Kane.

Johnny grinned as the thought struck him. Jake earned a passably good living for himself hunting or trapping predators and collecting bounties from the sheepmen, but there wasn't a livelihood for two in it.

His descending pick struck sparks from a boulder in his path. Patiently he began to loosen the earth around the boulder until he could sink the point of his pick beneath it and move it. Johnny pried the boulder out of its bed, bent down to clasp it with both hands, and heaved it out beside the ditch. Then he continued digging. It was hard, tedious, and slow work, with no diversions except that which Johnny could live in his own mind.

He found himself thinking mostly about Jake's red hound, Buck. The red pup had struck a chord in Johnny from the first. Buck had about him a quality that set him apart from other dogs, just as some people are set apart from others. It wasn't just a good nose, a fighting heart, or intelligence. Old Major had all those too and Buck still had something more. It was a characteristic that Johnny recognized without being able exactly to define. Part of it, he knew, was expressed in Buck's whole-hearted devotion to Jake.

Here, high on the red bluff, Johnny worked and thought and dreamed. One of his most cherished dreams was that Buck belonged to him, but of course that was impossible. Even if Jake would sell him— and he wouldn't for any price—Johnny couldn't just buy such a dog. The dog had to come to him, had to want him as a master, and Buck had already given himself whole-heartedly to Jake.

With the coming of night Johnny looked at the small amount of ditch he had already dug compared to the great amount he still had to dig, knew a discouraged moment, then swung his pick and shovel over his shoulder and walked down the bluff to the road. He had worked hard, but though his young muscles ached, he was not tired out. Reaching his grandfather's house, he was greeted by Allis with a chuckle.

"Ab says you've been working hard. He's been watching you."

Johnny grinned. "He wanted to make sure I wasn't goldbricking, huh? Well, I haven't been." He looked at his blistered hands. "Lord! There must be easier ways to earn a few dollars!"

"There's no easy way to earn anything," Allis grunted. "But Ab sort of thought you might need a helpful little push. He's already brought your three calves down."

"He did?"

"Yup. They're in the pasture."

"I'll go have a look at 'em!"

Without waiting to wash, Johnny ran down behind the house. Three Jersey calves, just old enough so that their horns were beginning to show, walked nervously about this unaccustomed pasture. Johnny examined them with a critical eye. Ab had been generous; he'd given Johnny good stock. But that was to be expected from Ab.

When Johnny entered the pasture, the calves moved shyly away from him. As Johnny watched delightedly, some magic balm seemed to ease all his aches away. No longer did the prospect of going back to work on the ditch seem tedious. He had his plans and they would work out.

A week after he'd entered the rimrock looking for the big lion, Jake Kane rode back out. His clothes were in tatters, he had a week's growth of beard, and he was so dirty that he felt as if his skin was crawling. Behind his saddle were tied the skins of a lioness and her two cubs, the three tawny tails dangling down the horse's flank. Jake had had to let the dogs run at last, and they'd treed the three lions in three different trees an hour and a half after they started them.

Jake stayed on the bridle path at one side of the highway, oblivious to the stares of the motorists passing by. Brakes squealed, tires shrieked, but Jake scarcely heard, for his mind was still up in the rimrock. For seven days he had searched it, covering endless miles and looking everywhere. He'd found bobcats, deer, elk, bears, and lesser lions. But there had not been the slightest trace of the big one he wanted, and that ground like a buzz saw at Jake's brain. He knew the big one must be there. It had to be, and at the very least he should have found its trail and his hounds should have run it, even though unsuccessfully.

When he came to Allis Torrington's place, he swerved into the yard and sat the saddle for a second. Tired as he was, a faint grin curled his lips. Something new had been added since Jake last saw the place, for three tail-switching Jersey calves stood in the fenced pasture. When Allis came out of his house Jake looked from him toward the calves.

"I see," he smirked, "that you're goin' to have a dairy."

"Ha!" Allis snorted. "You catch me milking a fool cow and you can put me out of my misery! They're Johnny's. He's going to feed 'em through the winter and, he says, sell 'em at a nice profit in the spring. Probably do it, too. If you was as smart as that kid, you might have amounted to something yourself. Where you been?"

Jake waved a hand that took in the whole rimrock. "Out yonder."

"See you got three."

"Yeah," Jake said gloomily.

"Why so sad about it? That's good bounty money."

"I missed the big one I was after, the one that hit Bud Caudell's sheep and Esteban Oregay."

"Couldn't find his trail?"

"Not a fresh one. I reckon Major's a little too old and the red pup just a little too young."

"Like me and Johnny, eh? What kind of hunter has that boy been, Jake?"

"For a kid he knows a lot. Give him another few years and he'll be good. Why?"

"He's fretting his heart out to go hunting but he's making himself work on that blasted ditch. If he'd been born fifty years ago, he'd have been a professional hunter."

"I know it. But you know as well as I do that there's no future any more for hunters like me. Don't let Johnny be a fool, Allis."

"He won't be," Allis promised. "He's going to go to forestry school and learn what goes on behind a desk as well as out in the brush."

Allis's two old hounds walked sedately around a corner of the house. Loftily ignoring Jake's pack, they sought a sunny spot and stretched out. Jake slid off his horse.

"What do you make of this lion, Allis?"

The old man shrugged. "He's not hard to figure."

"What do you mean?"

"Just this. Somebody chases or tracks a lion that acts in a certain way. Two or three more act the same way. The hunter compares notes with somebody else who's had lions do about the same things. So they make up their minds that all lions are pretty much alike. They're not. Sometimes you get an odd one, and that's what this one is."

"Did you ever know of a lion to act this way before?"

"Not just this way, but I've known two or three to go off the beam. Take a treed lion that's been hurt but gets away. He's going to be mighty leery about treeing again. He's going to steer clear of hounds and men and might take his hurt out on whatever he can. That could be why this one ripped into Bud's sheep."

"You mean it's possible for a lion to get a grudge against people?"

"All lions got that. It's just that most of them don't dare do anything about it. But this one does, and he's smart enough to get away with it—so far. How long you been after him?"

"A whole week," Jake said glumly. "I kept my dogs off enough bobcats and lions to stock every zoo in the country, partly because the sheepmen are standin' my expenses while I hunt and partly because I want to get him for personal reasons. I haven't forgotten Sally."

"He'll hit again," Allis said with conviction. "He'll keep on until somebody stops him."

"I'll stop him," Jake agreed grimly. "Be seein' you, Allis."

Jake rode home, unsaddled his weary horse, and patted him on the rump. The horse walked down to the stream, splashed across to join his mate, and fell to cropping the rich summer grass, while Jake carried his bundle of lion skins into the cabin. In winter he took only the scalps, but in summer there were always tourists who liked and bought every imaginable souvenir, and lion skins were very acceptable. If Jake left these at Connelly's store, Connelly probably would sell all of them.

Jake filled his teakettle, his dish pan, and as many other pots and pans as could be crowded on his stove, and built the fire up. He pulled a wash tub into the center of the floor, and when the water was hot he poured it into the tub. Stripping off his clothes, Jake climbed in, groaning with luxury as a week's accumulation of sweat and grime began to soak off. He soaped his back, and crooked his knees into the air so he could lie down and let his back soak while his head rested against the tub's rim. Finished, Jake rubbed himself briskly with a rough towel, then shaved.

He felt better as he began to mix a batch of biscuit dough. He'd carried very little food with him on the hunt. Fortunately he had discovered a lion-killed buck that provided fare for the dogs. Jake himself had made out with trout that he caught, varied with wild berries and fruit. Now he wanted civilized food, and after he'd mixed his biscuits he pulled some vegetables from his small garden. He thought of saddling his other horse and riding up to Connelly's for a steak or some pork chops, but that seemed like too much trouble. Instead he rigged a rod and caught himself three trout from the stream. He prepared and ate his meal and was just finishing when Bud Caudell's pickup truck rattled into the yard.

Bud came in carrying a sack against which frost crystals glittered, and dropped it on the floor.

"Sammy said you were past," he greeted, "and nobody's seen you since. Where've you been all this time, Jake?"

"Up in the rimrock."

"Any luck?"

"Got a lioness and three cubs. No sign of the big one."

"Couldn't get a line on him, eh? Well, I brought you some dog meat." Bud indicated the sack. "I've been here every second day to see if you were back yet, and when you didn't come I froze it. It's fresh."

"Thanks a lot. Those hounds can use it."

"You're going back to hunt the big cat?"

"Sure am."

"Good. He's got everybody worried now, and some of the herders won't keep their flocks in the back meadows where they think he's likely to show next. We have to get him."

"I'll sure try. How's Oregay?"

"Going back to his flock next week, with a revolver big enough to stop a rogue elephant. He says he hopes that the lion tackles him again. Esteban feels he has some revenge coming."

"Hope he gets it. Have somethin' to eat, Bud?"

"No thanks, I have to be getting along. Good luck."

"I'll need it. That's a right cagey cat."

All summer long Jake prowled the rimrock with his hounds. He knew it as no one else did, with the possible exception of old Allis Torrington, and his knowledge of lions was second only to Allis's. In order to achieve greater freedom of movement, much of the time he left his horse at home where he needn't worry about it. He poked into caves, walked ledges where a misstep would have sent him plunging a thousand feet to his death, scaled cliffs up which he had to haul his hounds with a long rope after he gained the summit. He did this by fashioning harnesses for them and leaving a loop in the shoulder strap. Then, with an iron hook on the end of his rope, he fished until he caught another hound.

He caught plenty of predators; the hounds would not have remained interested unless they were permitted to hunt now and again. They ran bobcats that mounted a pinon pine, or a rock, or sought refuge in caves from which the hounds dragged them, spitting and snarling. Or they treed tawny, rope-tailed lions, and when their prey was skinned the dogs ate its flesh while Jake caught trout in the streams, roasted bobcat on a green stick, or ate from his pack.

Throughout he had one great passion—to get the lion he was after. The big cat was still in the rimrock, and that Jake knew because he saw its paw prints in the sand or in the dust that blew in from the red rocks. Once he found its kill, a magnificent buck from which the lion had eaten, and then covered the remainder with brush and leaves. The kill was only a day old, and the hounds readily took the lion's trail. But they lost it at the base of a towering stone cliff that the lion could climb and Jake could not.

By the time he found a way around there was no trace of the lion on top. He seemed more than ever a spirit beast that could appear and disappear at will.

Every week Bud Caudell brought Jake meat for his hounds and every time Jake got his supplies at

Connelly's he charged them to Bud's account. The other three sheepmen were sharing this expense, and Jake never needed very much, but at the same time there grew within him a disinclination to let the sheepmen pay his way any longer. He had caught bobcats and lesser lions, and in one sense, even though he had not killed the big lion, he had paid his way by preventing any future sheep-killing by the cats he had caught.

That was where things stood when autumn snow clouds bridged the sky. Soon there would be snow on the ground, and everything that walked on it would leave a telltale message. Jake knew that if he could find the big cat's track on fresh snow, it would be a different story from the discouraging hunts of summer.

In the early darkness of a fall evening, Jake was eating his dinner when the hounds announced the arrival of a stranger. A few seconds later, Bud Caudell's truck stopped in Jake's yard. Jacketed and wearing gloves, Bud Caudell came in with a sack of dog food. His cheeks were pinched red by the outside cold, and a few flakes of snow clung to his jacket and hat.

"Winter's here," he announced. "Tracking snow by morning."

"I know it," Jake said. "Now I'll bring your damned cat in."

"You didn't get him last winter," Bud reminded him.

"My strike dog was pretty old and my best pup was too young. But the pup's as good as Major ever was, right now."

"I wish you luck," Bud Caudell said. "We don't want that cat around here when we bring our sheep back next season."

"He won't be."

Jake followed his visitor out into the falling snow. Already the yard was coated with white dust, and the tracks Bud had made coming in were half obliterated. Jake eagerly sniffed the brisk air, said good-bye to Bud, and went back into the house with real elation. He looked to his rifle, started to arrange his hunting gear, and then it occurred to him that tomorrow was Saturday. Johnny Torrington wouldn't have to go to school and probably would like to help hunt the big lion. Besides, Jake would like to have him along. Johnny was a good hunter and would be a real help. Jake put on his jacket and hat, went out again, and ordered the dogs back when they would have followed him.

He strode up the road through the swirling snow, liking its cold feel on his bare face and hands. Winter might be the hardest time of the year, but it was also one of the best times. Then the canyons and the rimrock belonged to those who lived in it, and was not crowded with those who did not. It was not that Jake resented vacationers, he just liked it better without them.

He saw Allis's window dully lighted through the falling snow, so Jake pushed the door open without knocking. Old Allis, sitting at the table before a half-eaten roasted chicken, greeted him heartily.

"Come on in, neighbor! Come in and fill your empty innards!"

Allis sliced a drumstick and second joint from the chicken, laid them on a plate, and filled a cup with coffee. Jake sat down willingly. Allis was a good cook, and it was seldom that Jake bothered to prepare for himself anything as elaborate as roast chicken.

"Where's Johnny?" he asked, his mouth full.

"In school," Allis rumbled. "There's some shindig or other going on, and he's gone with the Carews. They'll be in about ten o'clock. Got anything special on your mind?"

"There's a trackin' snow and I'm goin' after that big cat tomorrow. Think Johnny would like to go?"

"Ha!" Allis chuckled. "Try to keep him from it! That boy's almost as hound crazy as you are!"

"That's why I came. By the way, where's your hounds, Allis?"

"Batting around outside. They'll be pawing at the door in a minute or so."

Jake took a swallow of coffee. "Speakin' of hounds, that red one of mine is—"

The thin wail of one of Allis Torrington's old hounds, rising high above the wind, stopped him short. At the same time they heard the terrified bawling of Johnny's calves. Then came a high-pitched howl from the other hound, a sound of outrage and indignation. Before it had died, Jake was on his feet. He reached for Johnny's rifle, and Allis sprang up to seize his. Grabbing a flashlight, they ran outside.

The light ripped a hole in the darkness, but gently falling snow prevented its piercing through to the meadow. The two old hunters ran in that direction.

They found the calves where they had fallen, warm and bleeding. All three were dead. A little way beyond were Allis's two old hounds, stretched in the snow. They were dead, too, but in the almost toothless mouth of each hound was a patch of tawny fur. Ancient, rheumatic, and filled with pain though they had been, they had died as they had lived, in pursuit of predators.

"I knew it," Jake said. "Let's have the light."

He took the flashlight and went ahead to where scuffed snow was heaped in little piles. Jake knelt, looking at the tracks he found there, and was torn between rage and satisfaction. His old enemy had paid another visit, struck, and was gone. But this time he had gone in the snow.

"It's the big one, all right," Jake told Allis. "I'm goin' back, and get my hounds and rifle."

"Tonight?"

"I've got a fresh track tonight. When will I get another?"

There was something wistful in Allis's reply, something that said he knew he was too old. "I can't go with you, but hadn't you better wait for Johnny?"

"By the time Johnny gets here the track might be covered. I'm goin' to take it while I can."

Jake sped down the road toward his house, his mind on only one thing. His prayed-for opportunity, a fresh track on new snow, was here. If he did not put his hounds on it tonight, weeks or months might elapse before another such chance presented itself.

Hastily Jake made some sandwiches and stuffed them in the game pocket of his hunting jacket. He grabbed his rifle and two boxes of cartridges, and whistled the hounds about him as he raced back up the road, on into the meadow where the dead calves and hounds lay.

"All right," he ordered. "Take him."

The dogs left his side and sniffed away into the falling snow. Almost instantly Major's bellowing roar drowned the gentle night wind, then Doe's soprano tone blended with Major's, the bugle voice of Buck chimed in, and the bluetick's choppy bark. There was motion beside Jake and old Allis Torrington stood there.

"They've got it at last!" Jake said exultantly. "A fresh track on new snow! This time we'll have that killer's hide!"

"Still think you'd better wait for Johnny."

"There ain't time. Tell him I'll pay for those calves out of the reward money."

The hounds were running straight away, toward the rock country, and Jake swerved on a course that would take him quartering across the direction in which they were running. The snow fell harder, and the running hounds faded out of hearing. Jake did not worry. No man on foot, and very few horsemen, can keep pace with a pack of running hounds. But the chase would not continue to lead straight away. As soon as the lion got in the rocks he would probably circle. If Jake was lucky he could anticipate that circle, and close the distance between the hounds and himself. Failing that, he would simply have to plan as best he could and travel until he heard the pack. Then he would make new plans.

Jake turned again from his line of march, to head directly west, and in the darkness clambered up a rift in the rocks that he had climbed a hundred times. Reaching the summit, he heard the hounds again, faint in the distance.

Jake felt a rising conviction of success. The lion had had a long start and was running fast, but the hounds had his fresh trail and they would not lose it. The dogs went out of hearing again.

After listening for the hounds without being able to hear them, Jake broke the brittle lower branches from pines with his foot, gathered them up, and kicked a hole in the snow. Kneeling by the hole, he struck a match and lighted the little pile of twigs. When blue flame crackled through them, he added larger twigs. The fire made a flickering circle of light in the darkness, enough so that he could see and pile on larger branches. Falling snowflakes hissed quietly into the fire. Jake dozed, but awakened at periodic intervals to listen.

Dawn was creeping over the wilderness when, faint in the distance, he finally heard the yelping hounds. The noise swelled in volume as they drew nearer, and Jake speculated on the long hunt they must have had. Maybe they'd already been on the lion and failed to hold him; the big cat was very clever.

Then the hounds' voices all came from one place and Jake bounded to his feet. The dogs had their quarry at bay.

## 8

# Horse Cleft

Jake stood a moment, wanting to verify his hopes before he took any positive action. The lion was big and smart. He might have taken temporary refuge on a rock or in a tree from which he would leap and run away again, and Jake wanted to make no mistakes. It would accomplish nothing to go running off toward the yelling hounds if the lion was not really at bay. Jake would only have to wait for the dogs to run him down again.

The wind was strong and the voices of the hounds were very faint. But after he had listened for a few minutes, Jake identified clearly the voices of all four. If the lion had made any stands during the chase, or if there had been any fights, no dog had been killed.

After several minutes, certain that the big killer cat was treed at last, Jake started toward the hounds. He exulted with every step, full of the satisfaction of a man who sees a long and difficult job well done. For months he had been hunting this lion, and now at last it was his. Or at least as good as his. When Kane hounds treed their quarry, it did not get away from them. At the same time he felt a little of the uneasiness which this lion had inspired in him before. It was a devilishly clever cat and doubtless knew a trick or two that other cats didn't. Jake knew that he would have to watch himself very carefully.

He swung down a slope and climbed the other side of a forested, bowl-shaped depression. Then he was again in the rocks, and for a moment the tonguing of the hounds faded. Jake reached the rim of a ridge and the baying came clearly again. He tried by listening to locate exactly the place where the hounds had treed their quarry, and after a short space he thought he had it.

The lion had holed up in a long rock wall, known as Dead Man's Wall, that rose from eight hundred to a thousand feet above the surrounding broken country. It was marked by the usual clefts and fissures, and there were several caves in it. There were few trees on Dead Man's Wall, and the lion had probably taken to a fissure or cave. But that was all right; that he was at bay was the important thing. Jake had taken lions out of caves before.

The snow was deepening, so that it rose above his ankles, and there was no indication that the storm would lessen. But it would not hinder him seriously, either. Not now. As he went on, the swelling music of the hounds came loud and clear through the falling snow.

In his mind's eye Jake reconstructed Dead Man's Wall. He had climbed it fifty times in fifty different places, and now he tried by listening to the hounds to discover just where the lion had gone up. He began to feel a rising joy. Of all the clefts in the wall, only one had cliffs on both sides and a blind end that not even a lion could climb. It was Horse Cleft, inappropriately named, because no horse could go up or down it. Nor for that matter, could anything else. From the baying of the hounds, it sounded as though the lion had holed up in Horse Cleft.

Jake started to run. Bursting through a group of small pines, he verified his hopes. The lion had taken refuge in Horse Cleft. Jake halted to take stock of the situation.

At the mouth of Horse Cleft, where it emerged into the canyon, there was an eight-foot rock ledge which offered nothing except hand- and footholds. There were two caves in the cleft, a number of ledges and fissures, a few trees, and in the very center a rocky spire, seamed and worn, and perhaps forty feet from base to summit.

The hounds were trying to leap the rock ledge. But always they fell back in the snow and always, yelling, they tried again. Major's roar dominated the noise of the pack, with Buck's voice almost equal to his. In between came the choppy bark of the bluetick, and

Doe's shrill yelping. A smile of deep satisfaction split Jake's leathery face.

The lion had not only holed up, but he had done so in a place from which there was no possibility of escape. He couldn't go out the other end, and the hounds were guarding this end. Horse Cleft was no more than forty feet at its widest. And though a hound couldn't get into it, a man could. Jake reached down to pat old Major's head.

"We've got him," he said happily. "This time he's ours."

As Jake started to climb, a gusty wind bent the trees and sent snow flying, and Jake reached up to shelter his eyes. When he did, his foot slipped and he tumbled back down the ledge. His rifle flew from his hand, and he probed in the snow for it. Finding it, he brushed the snow from it with a gloved hand, ejected the cartridge, and blew through the bore. He squinted through and found it clean. Jake climbed back up the ledge and found the lion's tracks.

At first they were wide-spaced; the big cat had been leaping. Then, probably because he had discovered that the hounds could not get up here, he had slowed to a walk.

Jake grunted in satisfaction. Hunting, with him, was a business. It was the way he earned his living and he shot the predators his hounds brought to bay as a matter of course. Though he had never suffered any twinges of conscience about them, neither had he ever glorified the killing. But he knew that he would glory in the death of this cat because it was more than just a lion. It was a personal enemy, something that had wronged him, challenged him, and hurt him. It had hurt others, too, and would continue to be a menace unless it were destroyed. Carefully Jake followed along on the lion's tracks, and found where it had stopped to look back toward the hounds.

Jake went slowly, trying to see everything around him because he knew very well that he was hunting dangerous game. A misstep or a miscalculation could at the very least mean that the lion would slip past him. At the most, it would mean his death. The lion had already mauled Esteban Oregay; there was no reason to suppose that it would hesitate to attack other men.

Jake wondered about the big cat being here. If the lion had prowled this part of the rimrock extensively he should have known that Horse Cleft would be a trap for anything that entered it. Maybe the hounds had chased him clear out of the country with which he was familiar and he had never been here before. Yes, that must be it. The lion had entered a trap because he hadn't known he was going into one. He was far too wise to enter such a place knowingly.

Jake continued to move slowly, searching everything, and when a jay flicked its tail he whipped the rifle to his shoulder. A little sheepishly he brought it back down. He was keyed-up, nervous, and ashamed of it. This was no place for a case of nerves.

Following the track, Jake mounted a steep pitch and searched carefully around a stunted pine. He saw only a tufted-eared squirrel that ran along a branch, leaped to another one, and scampered into a hole. There was nothing else in the tree, nor were there any caves or holes hereabouts where a lion might hide. Holding his rifle with one hand, Jake started up another pitch. He kicked the snow away before seeking a foothold, for some of these slopes were treacherous when snow-covered. Fluffy snow sometimes bridged holes and fissures instead of falling into them, and to step into one unaware was to risk injury. Jake saw the lion's tracks leading straight to some dwarf cedars around another pine, and he eyed the spot carefully. But he saw nothing there. Jake began to worry. There were only four more trees in Horse Cleft, and if the lion was in none of them he must have gone into a cave or fissure. Getting him out might be something of a job, but it was a job that had to be done. Jake had trailed this lion over too many miles to have any thought of giving up the hunt now.

Suddenly he awakened to danger.

He saw the tip of the lion's ropy tail curled around a bit of brush at the base of the tree he had already searched. Jake whipped the rifle to his shoulder and with his thumb flicked the hammer back. He squeezed the trigger, and stared unbelievingly when he heard no report. He suddenly remembered that he had dropped his rifle.

Jake saw the cat leave the brush, its face a snarling mask in which bared fangs gleamed.

In winter it wasn't always possible for Chuck Jackson, the driver of Johnny's school bus, to keep a schedule. Winter in the rimrock was an unpredictable season, and though the roads might be plowed one hour they might be filled with new snow the next. On this Friday afternoon, with a storm in the making, Chuck left school right after dismissal time. Since his was the only bus that went down into the canyon, anybody not on it had to find his own way home.

Johnny and Bob Carew had stayed behind to appear in a play for the benefit of the football team, after which they were to get a ride home with Bob's father. After struggling through their lines, they sighed with vast relief, then hurried to the locker room to shuck off their costumes and put on their street clothes.

"How'd you like it?" Bob asked.

"The more I see of actors, good ones, the more I admire them," Johnny said firmly. "But I've made my first and last appearance behind the footlights."

"At least there weren't any rotten vegetables flying."

"Only because the audience didn't have any. How much did we gather in for Coach Weston's pride of the school?"

"I don't know, but it must have been plenty. People were standing in the rear."

"Probably because they couldn't hear the lines so well from back there. Say, listen to that wind!"

"I am listening to it!" Bob said unhappily. "And it means that tomorrow I'll have to help Dad hunt stormbound cattle!"

"Won't do you any harm to get your nose out of those books for a while," Johnny said smugly. "After all, you can get too much of one thing. Me, I'm going hunting. Jake Kane will certainly have his hounds out in this."

"Well, I wish I lived on a South Sea island," Bob grumbled. "Come on, let's go meet Dad."

When they went out, the street lights were soft and beautiful through the flying snow that half concealed them, sidewalks were ankle deep in snow, and a snowplow was churning along like some prehistoric monster. Johnny exulted. A born hunter, he loved hunter's weather such as this. Lions would be leaving their tracks in this snow, and Jake would surely want to go out. Maybe, Johnny thought, they'd even find the big one. But he had no real hope of that.

They reached the meeting where Bob's father, other stockmen, and representatives of the forest service were threshing out the various aspects of a new grazing program, and stood silently aside until the discussion was finished. Then they joined Mr. Carew for the snowy trip home. They rode silently through the quiet streets, the older man occupied with problems of the stockmen's meeting and Johnny and Bob weary from their play. Then the last lights of the little city glowed palely in the snow-wreathed background and they were in the pines. A herd of mule deer bobbed across the road, their eyes glowing pale amber in the car lights. They came to the long hill that took them down into the canyon, and finally to the gravel road that branched off toward Jake's and Allis's houses. Mr. Carew started down it, but Johnny stopped him.

"I can walk from here, and you might get stuck. Thanks a lot."

"You're welcome, Johnny. Good night."

"Good hunting," Bob called enviously.

Soft snow swirled around Johnny as he started down the road. As yet no track had broken it, and in the night it presented a beautiful curving pattern. As Johnny walked along, he thought of tomorrow's hunt, for certainly Jake Kane wouldn't miss this snow. In addition to the fun of hunting with Jake, Johnny always learned something new. Even though the day of the professional hunter was past, a knowledge of hunting and wild life would tie in with his work as a forester. Jake had told him of regions where almost all the bobcats, foxes and coyotes had been caught, only to have the same regions overrun with gophers, mice, and jack rabbits. And Johnny himself knew of one area where widespread predator control had backfired in a strange way. The authorities had nearly exterminated the bobcats, and after that the yucca cactus had failed to send its ten-foot-high flowers towering into the air. Investigation had proven that the yucca were pollinated by a certain kind of moth, and that the moths were being eaten by mice, which had multiplied when the bobcats were no longer eating them. Only when bobcats were again allowed to roam did the yucca start to bloom once more!

He was surprised when he came in sight of Allis's house to see a light there. Usually the old man went to bed shortly after dark and didn't get up until the sun was high. A little fear twisted Johnny's heart and he began to run through the snow. Maybe there was something wrong.

Johnny burst through the door and saw his grandfather sitting at the table. Allis seemed tired or unhappy, but he didn't look sick.

"Take off your things, boy," the old man rumbled. "Then warm your innards with a good hot cup of coffee."

Johnny took off his hat and coat, and kicked off his overshoes. As he sipped from the scalding-hot cup of coffee Allis had poured for him, he looked expectantly at his grandfather. For the first time, he noticed that the two old hounds weren't in their accustomed places near the stove. Allis cleared his throat.

"Johnny, that big lion hit again." The old man hesitated. "He got your three calves."

Johnny gulped. He thought of the many long, hot hours he had put in on Ab Whitley's ditch and of the numerous blisters that had helped pay for the three calves. Then he steeled himself and looked questioningly at the place where Pat and Sounder usually lay.

"He got them too." There was deep grief in Allis's voice. The old lion hunter's last two old hounds had been killed. Now there was nothing except himself left of the days he had known. "They were out prowling tonight when the lion came and they tackled him."

Understanding, Johnny said gently, "I'm awfully sorry, Grand Pop."

Allis shrugged. "Those things have happened before. They'll happen again, but not to me. Jake put his hounds on the lion's track and he's after him already."

"At night?"

"I wanted him to wait for you but he wouldn't. He said he had a fresh track on new snow and he might lose it if he waited. He's right, too. I'm sorry about the calves, Johnny. Wish we'd put 'em in the barn."

Johnny smiled ruefully. "So do I. Did Jake give you any idea where he was going?"

"Who knows where a lion's track will lead? All you can be sure of is that it'll head for wild and broken country."

"Do you think this is the same lion that's been raising all the other deviltry around here?"

"I'm dead certain it is."

"It just doesn't seem possible that one lion could hate people so that he'd take it out on them the way this one has."

"Don't fool yourself, Johnny. It's the same cat all right."

"Then he probably won't tree."

"I doubt it. Anyhow, he'll run a ways first. Jake's hounds were on him not fifteen minutes after he got your calves, so he wouldn't have much of a start. As soon as he got a chance, he'd try to break his trail so the hounds wouldn't be so hot on him, but he's done that before and he can do it again."

Johnny said wearily. "I'd better butcher the calves."

"I've already done it and skidded them into the barn."

"Then I'm leaving at daylight to see if I can find Jake and help him."

"Tracks will be gone. You'll have to go it blind."

"I know, but I might find him."

In spite of the fact that he was troubled about the loss of his calves, Johnny slept soundly and did not awaken until the alarm brought him leaping out of bed. He dressed hurriedly, tiptoed down the stairs, and looked sadly at the place where Pat and Sounder always slept.

Johnny built up the fire and shoved the coffeepot over to heat. He molded sausage patties with his hands, fried them, and ate breakfast. Then, tucking two sandwiches and a box of cartridges in his hunting jacket, he picked up his carbine and left the house.

Sometime during the night the storm had abated, leaving the ground heaped with seven inches of fluffy snow. The stinging cold that had followed it numbed Johnny's cheeks. He looked at the rimrock rising above him and felt a sense of helplessness. The country was so big, and a man and a pack of hounds were so small. The wind, blowing snow before it, had covered all tracks so effectively that there wasn't even a faint hope of tracking Jake. Johnny started into the meadows where his calves had been pastured.

Then he thought of his walk down the gravel road last night. The snow had been without a mark, and when Johnny came along there hadn't been enough wind to obliterate all tracks. Therefore the lion had not crossed the road; he must have gone into the country south of it. But where?

Johnny thought hard. Allis had said that the hounds were pressing the lion very closely, and that it would try to break its trail. The creek was the answer. Johnny remembered the old theory about cats disliking water, but he had known of some cats that even liked to swim. Besides, fear of water would not stop a lion hard-pressed by hounds.

But had the lion gone up or down the creek? Johnny stood for a moment, trying to find the answer. Then he started up the creek. Jake's house was downstream, and it was hardly likely that the lion, running from the scene of his latest raid, would set any course that might take him past a house. Besides, the nearest wild and broken country lay upstream.

Two hours after he left home, Johnny was hopelessly befuddled. He knew where he was and how to get back home, but so far there hadn't been even a faint sign that a lion and hound pack had come this way. They could be anywhere, and perhaps he was not within miles of any place they had been.

In front of him was the uneven, undulating line of Dead Man's Wall. Holding the rifle with one hand and seeking toeholds with both feet and his free hand, he climbed the wall through Pedunk Cleft.

Once on the top of Dead Man's Wall, he stood listening while the wind whipped about him. He was now uneasily certain of the fact that he was in error and had gone far astray, but the day was too far gone to seek a new route. Hearing nothing, he sought the lee of a boulder, built a small fire, and ate the sandwiches he had brought with him. He was sitting idly, enjoying the fire's warmth and speculating as to what he should do next, when faint in the distance he thought he heard a baying hound.

Johnny snapped to his feet, his jaw slightly open the better to hear. The wind made eerie noises as it whistled and moaned around the boulders and outjutting ledges. He thought he heard the hounds again, then figured that it was only the wind. Finally he heard the tonguing hounds clearly.

They were a long way off, but there was no mistaking Major's bass roar or Doe's shrill piping. Johnny kicked out his fire and began to run toward the sound. The hounds' tonguing came from one place; perhaps they had the lion at bay. Johnny listened for but did not hear the rifle blast that would tell him Jake had shot the cat. Possibly Jake was a long way off and had not yet located the hounds. In any event, it would not matter who shot this lion as long as somebody did.

Johnny finally came within sight of the hounds, but saw only Major, Doe, and the bluetick pup. They were not baying at any tree or pinnacle upon which the lion might have taken refuge, but instead were casting uncertainly back and forth. They seemed bewildered, as though they had encountered some situation foreign to them and did not know quite what to do about it. Coming nearer, Johnny saw what was troubling them.

They were at the edge of a long, deep chasm in the rimrock which they could not leap, but which would not be impossible for a lion. Though the hounds' running back and forth had eliminated most of the tracks on this side, the lion's paw prints were very plain on the other. Since there were no human footprints around, it was obvious that, somewhere in the rimrock, Jake Kane was looking for the hounds. Probably he was climbing high points and pinnacles, just as Johnny had done, the better to listen.

Old Major came dolefully up to Johnny and made whining little noises. As Johnny reached down to pat the old dog's head, he felt a great sadness. Buck was missing, and usually there was only one good reason why a hound should not be with the rest of a big-game pack. Somewhere during their long run the pack must have overtaken the lion, fought with it, and the red hound had been killed. Johnny's sadness gave way to anger. Of all the big-game hounds he had seen and would have liked to own, Buck was first.

Johnny said roughly, "Come on, Major."

The old hound, with Doe and the bluetick pup tagging close behind him, followed when Johnny led them way around the chasm. He took them back to the lion's tracks, and Major voiced a happy battle roar as the scent again filled his nostrils. The three hounds raced away and Johnny watched them go. He tried to calculate their line of travel, and ran to put himself in position in a cluster of pines so that he might get a shot at the lion should it circle back. But the hounds faded out of hearing and were gone.

Disconsolately Johnny climbed back down through Pedunk Cleft and began to make his way home. Allis was expecting him back and would worry if he did not come. But Jake could stay in the rimrock for as long as he chose. It was not unusual for him to be gone a week or more, even in winter. There was no reason to worry about Jake.

It was dark when Johnny got back. The old man looked at him questioningly.

"I didn't see Jake but I found the hounds," Johnny said. "That is, three of them." For a moment he did not speak. "The red one wasn't with the pack."

Old Allis shook his head. "He must have got in the lion's way. He was a real hound, too. Where'd you find the pack?"

"Up back of Dead Man's Wall. The lion had jumped a crack wide enough to stop the dogs. I took the other three around the crack and put them back on the lion's trail. Figured that doing anything else would only mix Jake up."

"It would," Allis agreed. "Jake should be able to pick 'em up again."

"How long do you figure he'll stay up in the rimrock?"

Allis shrugged. "As long as he figures there's a chance of getting that lion. Now that the lion's got his red pup, he'll be twice as mad as he was before."

"Reckon I'll go back for another look tomorrow," Johnny said. "It's Sunday and I won't have to go to school."

But, though Johnny went back up on the rimrock and stayed all day, he did not find a lion track, a sign of Jake Kane, or hear a hound.

# 9

# The Killer

When the dogs had first taken the lion's trail, he had broken it as Johnny guessed he might—by water. The big cat had jumped into the creek, waded it, and left the hounds temporarily at a loss until they worked out just what he had done and how he had done it. Then the dogs had become straightened out and resumed the chase.

Twice during that long first night they had bayed the lion. Once they had cornered him on a fallen tree that lay at the edge of a short but very deep chasm. The lion had faced them there, ears laid back, jaws framing a snarl, and the black tip of his tail twitching. When the bluetick pup came too near the lion had swiped at him with a front paw and knocked him ten feet into the snow. Had the blow landed squarely it would have killed the pup. But caution was another of the hounds' traits. They knew better than to come too near a lion such as this one and the bluetick pup had put himself in harm's way only because he was still inexperienced at close fighting. But the inborn agility of a Kane hound had saved him.

The lion had eluded the pack at this point by leaping across the chasm, which the hounds could not jump. They had to find a way around, and by the time they did the lion had a long start on them. But even though his tracks were snow-dusted, scent still clung to them and the hounds could follow.

The second time they brought him to bay was about an hour before dawn. The lion had climbed a rocky escarpment, and from it had jumped up a series of rocky little heads and outcroppings. Following close on his heels, and springing up, Buck ripped a chunk of skin from his underbelly. Enraged, the lion turned again to fight the hounds. He backed away from them, and when Doe rushed in to attack his rear, he whirled and struck her. For all his size the lion was incredibly fast. But Doe was far too smart to fall into any traps, and she escaped with only bruises. The lion started to run.

Covering twenty feet at each leap, he raced toward Horse Cleft, with the yelling dogs hot on his trail. He had been here only a couple of times before, and then when merely prowling from one range to another. Now he was looking for a ledge that he could climb and the dogs could not. The lion was tired and wanted to rest.

He scrambled up on the rocky ledge at the mouth of Horse Cleft while the hounds bayed wildly beneath it, and for a moment he looked back down on them. He was not afraid of the dogs, but it was no part of his creed to fight anything unless he felt like it. Without knowing that he had gone into a trap, the lion ventured a little way up the cleft, stretched out on a rocky ledge, and slept.

He was disturbed very little by the frantic dogs. They could yell and bay as much as they wished. At the same time, that part of a wild and hunted thing which must always be alert remained wakeful even while he slept. The lion sensed that eventually the yelling dogs would bring men, but he was not particularly afraid of them, either. When men came, he had only to climb Horse Cleft to its head and run on. He would then be rested, while the dogs would be worn out from their present mad efforts to reach him. The lion dozed fitfully.

He arose once to stretch and walk about, and again he glanced down at the yelling dogs. For a moment he considered leaping down on them. He might catch and kill at least one before it eluded him, but he knew the other three would attack him while he was doing it. The spot where Buck had ripped off the strip of fur was still dully painful and reminded him of what dogs could do. The lion lay down again.

Suddenly he came wide awake, for he knew that a man was coming. The lion had run across Jake Kane's scent before but he did not associate it with any specific incident. The lion stood still, testing the breezes that came to him and reading the man's approach by the wind. Then the big cat stretched leisurely, flexed his muscles, and started slowly up Horse Cleft.

Five minutes later he knew he had gone into a trap. The head of Horse Cleft, instead of being a narrow passageway through which he could escape, was a sheer, hundred-foot wall of rock worn so smooth that there was not so much as a single paw hold on it. The lion faced desperately back down the cleft, and tested the winds blowing up it. Jake had passed the hounds and was starting up the cleft.

In a frantic attempt to find a way out, the cougar glided to the side. There was no escape; the wall was sheer and unbroken. Rearing up, the lion looked toward the summit, then dropped to all fours and prowled nervously along.

When he was as close to Jake Kane as he dared get, he glided across the cleft to the opposite wall. That was smooth and unbroken, too. Desperation seized the big cat. He was trapped and he knew it.

Then the smoldering fires that had been kindled in his brain during the long months of his youthful captivity flared anew. He had had ample opportunity to study people, and he knew them as well as any wild thing can hope to. He knew also that he would have to fight his way out of this; there was no other course. His cunning brain began to figure out a course of action.

Though compared to a deer or a bear his nose was dull, compared to the average human's it was marvelously keen. The swirling wind currents told him exactly where Jake was and what he was doing, and the cougar planned well. At the base of a big pine there was a copse of dwarf cedar, and the big cat slunk into the cover. He flattened himself as he would for a rush at a deer, not letting even the tip of his tail twitch as he waited for the oncoming man. Then he saw him.

The lion watched, not moving a muscle as he waited. His great yellow eyes followed Jake, but he did not move because he sensed that so far he had not been seen. However, he knew exactly the second he was seen and sprang up and out as he would have at a deer. Even as he bore this man to the earth, fangs flashing, he felt the same awful fear within him that he had experienced at meeting a man during his raid on the flock of sheep. But this time he was driven by the desperation of knowing he was trapped, and did not panic as he had before.

Now, as he stood with one paw on his still victim, he somehow realized that men died very easily. Even a small deer would have put up more of a struggle than this man had. He sniffed curiously at Jake's body, sensing that the man was dead and harmless.

Down below the mouth of the cleft, the hounds were still leaping futilely at the ledge that prevented their ascending. Buck was as anxious as the rest to climb the ledge and be at the lion, but beyond that there was something that went deeper. From the very first he had loved Jake Kane with a whole-hearted affection, and now the red hound sensed that something was wrong.

He stopped tonguing and whined uneasily, as though that would somehow bring Jake to the head of the insurmountable pitch. When Jake did not come, the red hound rambled restlessly about. He tried to get up the ledge, climbed almost five feet, and knocked the wind out of himself when he fell back in the snow. Then he sat on his haunches, studying the wall. Had Jake not been in the cleft, he would have accepted the ledge as an unclimbable obstacle. But Jake was up there, and Buck had to reach his side.

The rock wall was almost perpendicular. But here and there were little outjutting knobs or warts. They began at one side and were irregularly spaced to within about eighteen inches of the top, where a six-inch shelf about two feet long thrust out from the wall. Buck tried again to climb, and when he missed this time he leaped into the snow instead of falling. For a moment or two, paying no attention to the other hounds, he wandered back and forth and reared against the ledge at various places.

The next time he started up he did not climb straight. Rather, he got a paw hold on an outjutting knob and reached sidewise to another one. For a second he teetered uncertainly and almost fell again, then righted himself and stretched his front paws to another knob. He brought his rear ones to them, bunching his feet together in the manner of a cat, and leaned against the rock wall to keep himself steadied. Bit by bit he climbed, angling back and forth wherever he could find a hold, and finally crawled up on the six-inch shelf. From there he stepped to the top of the ledge.

At once he rushed forward, his nostrils filled with lion scent, and saw the big cat standing over Jake. The lion's ears were laid back as he spat and snarled. Then, cat-like, his nerve broke suddenly. He streaked down the cleft and leaped from the ledge over the heads of the three dogs. Buck heard his pack mates thunder away on the lion's trail, and was mightily tempted to join them. But though he was not sure just what had taken place here, he was certain that something was very wrong. Instead of pursuing the lion he went softly to Jake.

One of Jake's arms was partially crooked over his face, and the red hound snuffled it uneasily. With a gentle tongue he licked Jake's face, and tapped at him with a paw behind which he put scarcely a feather's weight. With eager jaws Buck seized Jake's coat and pulled slightly. He whined.

When Jake did not move, the red hound lay very close to him, staring hard at his master. He turned his head and sniffed the lion's tracks. His hackles rose, but not because he saw any connection between the lion and the reason why Jake was lying so still. He simply didn't like lions, and he would have taken this one's track had not his first duty been to Jake.

The afternoon passed and night fell, and still the red hound lay beside his motionless master. He was very troubled and worried, for he loved Jake. Obviously something was wrong with him, for he had the smell of death that the dog had detected in other things. The red hound sat on his haunches and moaned his heartbreak to the uncaring sky.

In the morning a pine marten ventured near and Buck flew fiercely at it. He chased the furry little creature up a tree, and watched it make its way through the branches to another tree. The dog followed along beneath. Jake Kane lay dead in the snow, and the red hound was on guard. When the marten was chased safely out of sight, Buck returned to Jake.

All through the day, night, and the next day and night the dog maintained his vigil, eating nothing and licking only a little snow to satisfy his thirst. He burrowed into the falling snow so that he might stretch himself very close to Jake. From time to time he moaned fitfully. Jake was stiff and cold, and the red hound had seen many things that were that way. They had never walked again. Little by little, a resolute hatred grew in the dog.

The red hound's brain was not that of a human's; he was unable to reason cause and effect between Jake's meeting the lion and his death. However, Buck had elemental knowledge of hunts, and life, and death. He knew that Jake had been alive when he met the lion, and he had seen the lion standing over Jake's body. He instinctively felt a connection, and the red hound's anger became a fierce, hot rage. With a last long, wailing moan, he left Jake's side, leaped from the ledge up which he had climbed so painstakingly, and set off into the snow-locked wilderness.

The scent of the lion and the other three hounds had long since faded, and he hadn't the least idea of where to go. But in his heart was a burning resolve. The will to hunt was born in him, but now Buck wanted to hunt just one thing. Somehow and somewhere he must again find the lion that had met Jake Kane in Horse Cleft. When he did, he would fight the big cat.

Chance alone took him up through Pedunk Cleft and to the top of Dead Man's Wall. He loped through the snow, not hurrying because in his world there was need for hurry only occasionally. When he came to a lion-killed deer he ate from it, then curled up beside the kill and slept. The lion that had made the kill, and that had failed to make another, came back to it for another meal. The red hound faced him, bristling. When the lion faded back into the trees, Buck did not chase it. Ordinarily he would have tongued happily on the trail, but now he wanted only one lion.

The next day he trotted on through the snow, and came to a grove of aspens growing among the pines.

Mule deer bounced away as the the red hound coursed along their paths. He did not chase them or think of chasing them, for he was a big-game hound whose training and instinct told him that he must hunt cats. It never occurred to him that he might pull down his own game and he did not try to do so. But there were enough lion kills about so that he did not go hungry.

Nor did he lack for lion and bobcat scent. In the aspens he found where a lioness with two half-grown cubs had been lying on a sunny ridge. The place was littered with deer hair and bones, and reeked of cat odor. Buck sniffed about, his interest quickening, but he did not follow the trails that led away from the lair for he had no interest in these lions. He found another place where a male lion had established a regular beat, and the dog chased him a half mile until he treed. For twenty minutes he bayed the tree, but only half-heartedly.

After three days Buck went back to Horse Cleft and, as he had done before, zigzagged up the rock wall. He curled up in the snow very close to where his master lay, knowing some measure of contentment. It was comforting just to be near Jake.

He stayed throughout the day and left, again to prowl the rimrock in his restless search for the big lion. He had no thought of abandoning the hunt. He must find the lion, and when he did he would fight him. That had become his consuming ambition. But though he ran across the tracks of several smaller lions, he did not find the big one he sought.

When the lion sprang over the heads of the three hounds at the mouth of the cleft, he did not stop to fight them. Instead, he leaped to a ledge on Dead Man's Wall, ran up it, and climbed until he had mounted the wall. There he turned again to listen for the hounds.

He heard them tonguing, but they were still at the bottom of the wall and at least for the time being they had been left behind. The lion started into pine forest on top of the wall, a sense of power rising within him over what he had done. Men no longer seemed the super creatures he had always considered them. The one in Horse Cleft had died as easily as the two old hounds.

A savage, vicious beast, ten times as dangerous as he had ever been before, the big lion continued into the forest. Though he knew he would never, of his own free will, face humans in daylight, he was no longer afraid of them. Should any more get on his trail, he would know how to deal with them.

He had not gone more than a mile when he heard Major, Doe, and the bluetick, who had found a way to get up the wall, tonguing hotly on his trail. The lion turned to listen, snarling. He did not particularly fear these hounds, but they did pose a threat, and they annoyed him.

The lion was rested now, and he broke into a run. He was not very familiar with this area; the hounds had driven him out of country where he knew every ledge and crevice. Now the lion hurried to get back to a place he knew well. He came to the long, deep chasm in the rimrock, and turned for a desperate stand.

For a half hour the fight surged back and forth, with the hounds going in to rip at the lion whenever an opportunity presented and the lion trying to pin one of them down. Unable to do it, he leaped across the chasm and ran on. He was nervous, for he was sure that the hounds would come again. When he did not hear them, he slowed to a walk. The lion stalked and killed a deer, and was about to eat from his kill when once more he heard the hounds. He started to run. He reached a tumbled mass of rocks just as the three yelling hounds broke from the forest and were upon him. The lion turned to face them. He waited until they swept close, and when they were near enough he lunged at Major.

He missed. Though he was old, Major had faced so many lions that he knew them well and could tell what they were going to do next. When the lion charged, Major slipped to one side while Doe and the bluetick bored in to slash at the lion's rear. He snapped around to face them, and struck the bluetick a glancing blow that knocked the wind out of him. When the lion tried to follow up, Major and Doe were at his flanks.

He struck again, angry and frustrated. Physically, he was more than a match for all three dogs at the same time. They knew it, and kept out of his way. Their function was to worry and hold the lion, and to do as much damage as they could while holding him. Major slipped in, sliced a mouthful of skin from the lion's flank, and was away before there could be a return strike.

The lion ended the fight. Turning, he bounded to the top of a rock and from there to a ledge on a bluff. Trotting along it, he found paw holds that nothing except a lion could find, and went into forest on top of the bluff. Turning to listen for the hounds, he could not hear them, so he loped easily through the snow and dropped down a slope to a cedar canyon where he knew he would find deer. He had not had a chance to eat and was very hungry.

Once in the cedars he slunk along, belly scraping the snow as he watched for a deer. He saw two big ones feeding, and lay perfectly still while they fed nearer. When they were close enough, he made his rush. He overtook the biggest deer, a buck that had shed its antlers, and leaped astride it. The buck fell to its knees in the snow, struggling furiously until the lion's teeth met through its spinal column.

The lion stood a moment over his kill, twitching his tail, amber eyes glowing. Then he fed ravenously, tearing off as much meat as he wanted and covering the rest with sticks and brush. Always he preferred fresh-killed meat, and should he make another kill he would not return to this one. But if hunting was poor and he did not kill again, he would come back here when he was hungry. His belly full, the lion traveled a short distance to a thicket and curled up to sleep.

He had slept scarcely twenty minutes when again he heard the yelling hounds on his trail. The lion bared his fangs in an angry snarl, raced to a nearby canyon, and climbed a ledge just ahead of the dogs. From there he clawed his way to a higher ledge, one that was rimmed by brush. The lion looked down on the frantic hounds and up the bluff above him.

Wind currents blew strongly to him here, and the wind carried no scent of man. The lion would have much advance warning should one come, and he could escape if he cared to do so. But he was no longer certain that running away from men was desirable. From this ledge he could easily leap onto any man who walked beneath it. He stretched out behind the brush.

The yelling hounds still made him uneasy, and after an hour the lion got up to climb the bluff. On the top, he stood with his nose into the wind and his ears alert. He could not hear the hounds, and that made him feel a little easier.

It was well into the next day before the hounds found him again. The lion sprang up from his bed, spitting his rage at these pursuers who would not let him rest. He had tried and failed to kill them, and experience had taught him that was largely because there were three of them. When he tried to attack one, it eluded him, and when he pounced after it he had to defend himself from the other two. All the lion could do was run, and that inflamed his temper.

Once more the lion climbed, and once more the hounds discovered a way around and were upon him. The chase see-sawed back and forth across the rimrock, with the lion working farther away from familiar country and never knowing peace. He mounted another pinnacle, saw the dogs sweep in beneath him, and ran on.

He ran nervously now, trembling and afraid, for he was sure the hounds would come again. He did not know that this time, too weary, too hungry, and too footsore to trail any more, they had finally turned back. The lion knew only that they had clung to him like leeches, and he traveled fast and far.

The hounds had been on his trail almost a week, and another week passed before the lion began to relax. His were the nerves of a cat, always explosive, always set on hair trigger. Even though he had not heard them for a week, from every kill and resting place he listened for the hounds. Then finally he heard a hound tonguing.

Deep and steady, the sound rose above the winter wind. The lion listened intently. There had been four hounds on his trail originally, but only three had followed over the long chase. Now the lion knew where the fourth one was; it was on his trail and coming fast. The tip of the lion's tail twitched angrily. He had failed to kill any hounds before because there were three.

Now there was only one.

# 10

# Lost Trail

All week long Johnny fretted in school, and because his mind was not on his studies, he did not do so well in them. This brought reprimands from two of his teachers and Johnny made an earnest effort to buckle down and study. But though his body was in school, his spirit and thoughts were up in the rimrock with Jake Kane. Jake had not come home, which could mean only that he was still relentlessly hunting the big lion.

Johnny heaved a grateful sigh of relief when Friday afternoon finally came and Chuck Jackson's bus was pulling out of the school yard.

"Whew!" he said to Bob Carew. "This has been the longest week of my life!"

"It didn't do your teachers any good, either," Bob observed. "What are you going to do? Take a few courses over again next year?"

"Aw, I'll get going again."

"You didn't make a passing mark all week. Has it ever occurred to you that Jake Kane can take care of himself? He did it quite a few years before he had you to worry about him."

"I'm not worried about him. I just want to know how he's doing."

"What's so fascinating about a bunch of mangy mutts yapping after an overgrown house cat?"

When Johnny did not answer, Bob stopped needling him, and said no more until the bus slowed for Johnny's stop.

"Good hunting, fella," Bob said understandingly.

"Thanks."

Johnny swung from the bus and hastened down the trodden path toward home. He burst into the house and looked hopefully at his grandfather. The old man shook his head.

"No word yet, Johnny."

"Lord! Wonder if he aims to spend the winter on the rimrock?"

Allis shrugged. "He'll be back, but not as long as he figures there's a chance of getting that lion."

"I didn't think hounds could run this long."

"They can't; they have to rest and eat. But they don't need too much rest before they can go on again. Those are Kane hounds."

"Even Kane hounds have to play out some time."

"They will," Allis assured him. "Why don't you go over to Jake's in the morning? He's been gone a long while and he may come in during the night."

"That's a good idea."

After they had eaten, Johnny made an earnest effort to devote some concentrated attention to his neglected studies. Allis went to bed and a half hour later Johnny followed. An hour and a half before dawn, he awakened to the strident clatter of his alarm clock. Johnny dressed, washed, breakfasted, and with his rifle under his arm stepped into the cold of a winter morning.

The north wind fanned his cheek lightly. Stars and a wan sickle of moon glowed palely against a sky so clear that there was not even a faint trace of haze. Frost glittered and the snow was crisp under his rubber pacs.

As he neared Jake's house, Johnny could neither see nor smell smoke, and knew that Jake had not come home. He swung on his heel and started back up the road.

He stopped suddenly, thinking he'd heard something, and brought the rifle into position for a quick shot. A cold shiver fluttered up his spine and Johnny shook his head in irritation.

"I've sure got lion jitters," he muttered.

Then he swung to look back down the road and saw old Major following him. About fifteen feet away, Major stopped silently with his left front paw upraised. He shivered, and his tail drooped sadly. A hound's face always looks mournful, but on Major's now there was also a look of desperate weariness. In the early morning light Major almost seemed to be crying. Still holding his front paw clear of the snow, Major limped up to Johnny and gravely touched him with a cold nose.

"You poor mutt!" Johnny said in a burst of sympathy. "What's happened to you?"

The battle-scarred old hound was incredibly gaunt. Jake's hounds hunted so much that they were never fat, but Major's every rib showed plainly against stretched skin and Johnny's two hands would almost have encircled his paunch. The old dog's hip bones were like two blunt clubs thrust above his rear legs. Even his tail was a mere wisp made unsightly by long, protruding hairs.

Johnny clasped the old hound to him, stroking his head while fear welled up in his heart. Jake couldn't have come home; he never would have left a hound in this terrible condition out in the snow. But where was he? Major walking slowly beside him, Johnny went back to Jake's house.

He found Doe and the bluetick, almost too exhausted to move, sleeping in the same kennel. Doe raised her head to look at Johnny, touched his hand with a cold nose, sighed, and stretched herself out. The bluetick wagged an apathetic tail. Doe and the pup were as emaciated as Major, and more tired. Even their toenails had been worn away to mere stubs and their pads were raw. Wherever they'd been, certainly they had run for endless miles.

Johnny went to Jake's house, opened the door, and walked into the dank chill of an unoccupied kitchen. There had been no fire in the stove and there were no cooking utensils on it; Jake's pots and skillets hung on their usual row of nails driven into the wall. Johnny walked across to the bedroom and opened the door. The bed had not been used.

As he went slowly out of the house, Major met him at the door, whining uneasily. Johnny brushed a hand across his sweating forehead. The hounds were back and Jake was not. That must mean that he was dead; the hounds would not have left their master had he been alive. But first things must be first, and right now the hounds needed attention.

Major limped slowly beside him as Johnny returned to the kennel where Doe and the bluetick lay. He coaxed them gently.

"Come on. Come on out."

The bluetick, acting like an old and very tired dog, came slowly out and stood shivering. Doe tried to get to her feet, stumbled, slid out of the kennel door, and Johnny caught her as she fell. He eased her down into the snow and Doe rested her head on his knee. Cradling her in his arms, Johnny picked her up. Doe had run so long and fed so little that she seemed to be only half her former weight.

Awkwardly carrying both Doe and his rifle, Johnny started slowly up the road. Then he slowed even more, for Major and the bluetick were hard pressed to walk at all. Johnny turned in to Allis's house, pushed the door open with his knee, and kicked a rug across the floor to the stove. He laid Doe on it. Major and the bluetick sighed gratefully and lay down near the stove. Johnny put his rifle back on its rack and knocked at Allis's door. Ordinarily the old man liked to sleep until he was ready to get up. But this was an emergency and Johnny wanted advice. He heard Allis stirring.

"What do you want? Anything wrong?"

"Three of Jake's hounds came home last night and Jake didn't."

"I'll be right out!" Allis said quickly.

A moment later, shuffling in slippered feet and tightening his belt, Allis came from his room and looked at the three hounds.

"Warm some milk, Johnny," he ordered.

Johnny poured a quart of milk into a pan and put it on the stove. Allis took a skillet from the nail where it hung, went into the storeroom for a package of lard, and sliced a chunk into the skillet. Then he knelt beside each of the three hounds in turn, running experienced but gentle hands over them.

"They're not hurt," he announced, "just run out. How's the milk coming?"

Johnny tested it with a finger. "Getting warm."

"We don't want it hot." Allis took three bowls from the cupboard and poured an equal portion of milk into each. Major and the bluetick stood on shaky legs to lap up their portions. Kneeling beside Doe, Allis held her head so she could drink. Finished, all three hounds sighed and lay down. Allis gathered up the empty bowls.

"That'll be enough for a while," he said. "Those hounds haven't had much to eat and we'll have to take it easy before we can get 'em back on red meat. They're not going to do any hunting for a spell, either."

Johnny asked the question that he'd been avoiding. "Is Jake dead?"

"Don't jump the gun," Allis advised. "It looks as though he may be, but we don't know. He's either hurt or dead. Jake wouldn't get lost in the rimrock."

"If he's just hurt, why are the hounds home? They wouldn't leave him."

"Take it easy, Johnny. Those hounds have been gone a week and Jake might have been hurt in the hunt. When the dogs got hungry and footsore enough, they could have come home instead of going to look for Jake." He began to soften the hounds' worn, raw paws with melted lard.

"Could the lion have got him?" Johnny asked.

"I doubt it. Lions don't kill people. Jake might have been caught in a slide, or fallen into a chasm that he didn't see because it was bridged by snow, or slipped on an icy cliff. There's any number of things that might have happened."

"Don't you think we should organize a search party?"

"Of course. We'll do it on the chance that Jake's still alive and able to start a fire that can be seen. But think of what you're saying, Johnny. The rimrock's a right big place. If Jake's dead, and maybe buried under an avalanche or at the bottom of a 50-foot chasm, who would know he was there? And if he wasn't caught in a slide or fall, there are still a few thousand places that a whole army of searchers could pass and never see him at all."

"We could narrow it down," Johnny pointed out stubbornly. "What time did Jake leave here when he took after the lion?"

"About half past six."

"Well, next day, a little after noon, I found the hounds at that crack just this side of Alligator Head. Jake has to be some place between here and there."

"Does he?" Allis grunted. "You don't know that Jake wasn't looking for the hounds when you found them, or what kind of trail that cat laid between here and Alligator Head. Still, there might be something in the idea. You go up in the rimrock and start looking. I'll roussle the boys out for a search party, and keep an eye on these hounds."

All the rest of that day and all the next Johnny searched the rimrock, concentrating his efforts on that part between Allis's house and the place where he had found Jake's hounds. He climbed pinnacles, points, and bluffs, searching for the telltale plume of smoke that would reveal a campfire.

There were none, and Monday morning Johnny went reluctantly back to school. Still the search went on. Every man in the canyon who could get into the rimrock did so, looking for Jake Kane. Volunteer pilots flew over, bringing their planes as low as they dared, while they searched intently for the campfire that would tell them an injured man was there. By the end of the week even the most optimistic of the searchers had abandoned hope. Jake Kane certainly was not alive, and if his body was ever found at all, it would be accidental. As Allis had said, there were numberless places where searchers might pass within yards of a dead man and never see him.

On Friday night Johnny sat disconsolately at the kitchen table, facing Allis. Outside, old Major scented something, and growled a challenge at it. Doe barked sharply and the bluetick joined in. The hounds were recovering, but were still footsore, and would not be able to hunt for a while.

"There wasn't even a trace?" Johnny asked.

"Nary a sign, Johnny, and the boys have been all over the place. They've looked wherever anybody could think of looking."

"But they haven't looked everywhere."

"If they had, they'd have found Jake. Be reasonable, Johnny. They might comb the rimrock for a year, or ten years, and still never find him. Jake isn't the only man lying out there."

Johnny said dejectedly, "I know, but I'd like to have another try at it anyhow."

"Go ahead," Allis urged. "At least you'll satisfy yourself."

"I know that, but there's still a chance."

The next day Johnny went into the rimrock, but this time he varied his searching procedure. There was no use in climbing high points and looking for a campfire; if there'd been any fire, some of the searchers would have found it. Johnny poked into caves and fissures, searched ledges on steep-sided canyons, looked into thickets, tried to find recent snowslides, and even used a long stick to probe deep, unfrozen pools. He found nothing at all, but at dawn the next morning he stubbornly headed back into the rimrock again.

It was a tremendous undertaking and he knew it. He also knew that no one man, or any dozen men, could possibly have examined every place in the section he'd chosen yesterday. But Johnny had searched as thoroughly as he could. This morning, still working the area between Allis's house and the crack where he'd found the baffled hounds, he swung a little farther north.

Noon found him on the side of a forested canyon with gently sloping walls, and Johnny sat down to eat his lunch. He was just starting his second sandwich when, in the distance, he heard a tonguing hound.

He sat alert, listening but not believing. Many dogs sound alike, but few have voices that are exactly the same. The tonguing hound sounded like Buck, but it couldn't possibly be.

Five minutes later Buck came in sight.

The red hound was running down the opposite wall, about two hundred yards up the slope, and if he continued on his present course he would pass Johnny about three or four hundred yards away. On the point of running across the canyon to see if he could intercept the dog, Johnny was suddenly rooted where he sat.

Directly opposite, a big pine was surrounded by a bushy fringe of small trees all the way from a few inches to four or five feet tall. As Johnny looked, he saw a big lion leave that cover and run to the shelter of another tree about twenty yards farther on. The lion crouched there, and so expert was he at hiding himself that, after he stopped, he could not be seen at all.

Johnny figured there could be only one reason why the lion was hiding and not running. He knew the hound was on his trail and intended to ambush it. Johnny lay prone and rested his rifle over the grained back of a boulder. He sighted on the place where the lion crouched, but even as he did so he felt the hopelessness of his situation.

His rifle was a carbine, sighted in for a hundred yards, and the lion was probably three hundred and fifty yards away. Even under the best of circumstances, that was a very long distance for any except the most expert marksmen, and they did not use carbines. Johnny relaxed his tense belly muscles and cocked his rifle, hoping the lion would come into sight before the dog arrived.

Buck was coming fast, and there was a rising note of excitement in his voice as the trail freshened. Johnny waited, knowing that he would have to gauge his timing precisely. A pack of dogs could hold a lion even if they didn't tree him, but one lone dog stood almost no chance. Since Johnny couldn't see the lion yet, he would have to shoot at the exact instant the big cat broke cover. When they started fighting, they would be so close together that the chances of hitting the hound would be equal to those of killing the lion.

Buck came closer to the lion's ambush, and still closer. His head was up now; he was running by body instead of trail scent. He evidently knew where the lion was for he sounded a fierce, thundering challenge. Then the lion left his tree and bounded forward.

The lion was not a good target, only a flitting, tawny shadow that arched through the air. Trying to keep cool, and to correct as well as possible, Johnny sighted a full eighteen inches over the lion's back and squeezed the trigger.

At the report of the gun, the lion whirled and raced uphill. He was a dodging, racing shape among the trees, seen clearly only occasionally and briefly when he flitted from behind one tree and leaped across the small open spaces to another. Johnny shot again, and again, emptying his rifle as the lion ran and knowing as he did so that his shooting was wild.

The lion ran swiftly toward a rocky escarpment on the canyon. There he disappeared, with Buck hot on his trail. Hastily Johnny filled his rifle's chamber with more cartridges and levered one into the breech.

Now the red hound was tonguing steadily and furiously near the base of the rocky bluff. Leaving the rest of his lunch where it lay, Johnny ran down the slope. Reaching the pile of almost sheer rock that the lion had climbed and that Buck was trying to, Johnny looked wonderingly at the dog.

The red hound was thin, but he was not gaunt; evidently he had been eating with fair regularity. Though his nails were worn, Johnny could see as he reared against the rocks that his pads were not raw. In contrast to the pitiable three that Johnny had found at Jake's house, he seemed to be in good condition. Puzzled but delighted, Johnny knelt in the snow.

"Here, Buck," he said eagerly.

Seeming to be aware of Johnny's presence for the first time, the red hound dropped to all fours and looked at him. His eyes were not those of a dog at all, but of a ferocious wolf. He bristled, and his lips lifted from gleaming ivory fangs. He lunged fiercely, and Johnny dodged aside.

Without stopping, the red hound ran at full speed, along the base of the bluff, on into the forest.

# 11

# The Feud

For a moment Johnny stayed rooted, too astonished to move. Buck was a big, powerful dog, and had the red hound attacked him instead of running away, it would have been a nasty situation. But why had Buck displayed any hostility at all? And then why had he run away?

As Johnny tried to analyze the dog's action, he succeeded only in baffling himself further. His first reaction was that Buck had turned wild, and that he never would be otherwise. Then he realized that the hound had seemed more insane than wild. Buck had known that the lion was waiting for him. A pack dog, he also knew that only a pack of dogs could fight a lion that chose to make a stand on the ground. Yet he had seemed about to attack the big cat alone. If he had done so, if Johnny's shot had not frightened the lion, there would be little question but that the hound would have been killed.

What should he do? The lion had escaped over the bluff, and the dog had run around it, probably looking for a way up. By the time Johnny could climb up himself, lion and dog would be miles away. Suddenly he decided to return home and tell his grandfather about it. Allis would have some explanation.

Halfway down the slope he halted, thinking he heard Buck tonguing again. But it was only the wind in the canyon pines. Johnny crossed his fingers, thinking of how close the lion had come to killing the red hound.

"Hope he can't find that big cat again," he murmured to himself.

He reached the road, walked down it, and swerved toward home. The three hounds in the yard rose with wagging tails and friendly whines of greeting when he appeared, but for once Johnny had no time for them. He entered the house to find his grandfather preparing a pot of stew. The old man looked at him in surprise.

"Back so soon?"

"Jake's red hound is still in the rimrock!" Johnny blurted.

"You saw him?"

While Allis listened intently, Johnny gave a complete account of the incident. For a moment the old man said nothing. Then he questioned Johnny closely.

"You're sure this red hound wanted to tear into the lion?"

"That's all he wanted."

"And he snarled at you when you tried to catch him?"

"He looked as though he could have killed me!"

"But he didn't bother you after you got out of his way?"

"No. He just ran on. What do you make of it?"

"This red hound, he was all for Jake, wasn't he?"

Johnny nodded glumly. "He was strictly a one-man dog, and all Jake's."

For a full two minutes Allis's old eyes stared at the frosted window, while Johnny said nothing. The old man finally turned to him.

"Johnny, this is all guesswork. But I've seen some hounds in my day, a lot of them good hounds. Now bear in mind that I don't know, but from what you've told me I'd say the lion got Jake."

"You would!"

"Think about it yourself, Johnny. Jake disappears. Three of his hounds show up and the fourth doesn't. Jake was hunting a lion that's known to be big and mean. Then you find the fourth hound, the red one, and his only aim is to kill the lion. He is also, it seems, willing to fight anything that tries to stop him. What's it look like to you?"

"I didn't know dogs could think that way!"

Allis said quietly, "I didn't say they could *think*

that way. But there's still a mite you can learn about dogs. And that red hound isn't ordinary. If he liked Jake that much, and figured the lion hurt him, he might go after him. Mind you, it's still guesswork. But if we're guessing right, Jake does lie somewhere between here and Alligator Head. I think it'd be a piece up in the rimrock; that lion would have run a ways before he turned."

"But there were only three hounds at the crack near Alligator Head."

"That's why I think the lion might have got Jake soon after they started. If Jake was lying in the snow somewhere, that red hound would have stayed with him, at least if he was alive. Only afterwards would the dog get the idea of taking off after the lion. That's why there were only three dogs, or at least that's what I think."

"Then there's no hope of Jake's still being alive?"

"Not now. And finding his body is going to be hard, unless we can somehow tame that red hound and maybe get him to lead us to Jake. But that lion comes first. If he's killed Jake, he'll kill again. We've got to get him."

"We?"

"That's right, Johnny. Some of my joints could stand oiling, but I can still get up into the rimrock if we take it easy and don't try to gallop all the way."

"When do we start?" Johnny asked eagerly.

"Whoa there! We'll get nothing but a misfire if we

go off half-cocked. We need the hounds and they still need rest. Start them now and their pads would be worn through again in half a day. We'll have to wait until they can hunt."

"When will that be?"

"Maybe another week."

Johnny asked anxiously, "What about Buck?"

"He's been lucky this far. Maybe his luck will stay in and he won't catch up with that big cat again."

Johnny had a vision of the red hound, alone in the rimrock, pursuing a blood feud with the beast that had killed his master, and swallowed a lump. Buck had loved only Jake, but Johnny loved Buck, and was worried about him.

"Don't you think we could get him and bring him in?"

"You can try if you want to, but think of what you're saying. Of twenty men who've been in the rimrock, you're the only one who's seen that red hound. Maybe that's because he hasn't been tonguing. Or it could be because the lion's been laying some mighty lonely trails. You're going to have a rough job just finding that dog again. If you do find him, from what you've told me you'll have to beat him down before you'll be able to bring him in. How do you aim to do that?"

"I hadn't thought."

"Well, I can't tell you, but even if you can bring him in the chances are that we'll have an outlaw on our hands. I think Buck wants that lion dead. He's not going to be satisfied until it is dead. The best thing to do is leave him where he is and hope he's lucky. If we get the lion, we'll get the dog, too. You wait and see."

"I'd sure like to get Buck."

"You really think a lot of that hound, don't you?"

"An awful lot. Besides, if we had him we'd have Jake's whole pack. Saturdays and Sundays I could sort of take up where Jake left off and hunt lions and bobcats for bounty money."

"You won't get rich doing that, but . . . say, isn't there a big bounty on that cat?"

"That's right. Five hundred dollars."

"You could use that for forestry school. Anyway, I sort of have an idea that Jake would like for you to have his hounds. But you've got to wait until they can hunt again. Right?"

Johnny thought again of Buck alone in the rimrock with the big killer cat. He said reluctantly, "All right, Grand Pop."

When the lion climbed the rocky bluff he was seething with fury. Without suspecting that a man was even near, he had laid what seemed a certain ambush for the red hound. Then Johnny's bullet had smacked into the frozen ground six inches downslope from him. His reaction was instantaneous. At top speed he raced toward the rocky escarpment, twisting and dodging among the trees.

However, though Johnny did not know it, not all of his shots had gone wild. One had plowed through the fleshy part of the lion's right shoulder, and while it was not a serious wound, it was painful. It did not interfere with the lion's ability to climb, but it both enraged him and slowed him somewhat. Scrambling to the top of the bluff, he ran through open forest toward a higher bluff about a quarter of a mile farther on.

It was an old and proven strategy. The lion could climb to ledges that nothing except another cat was able to reach and he knew that by so doing he could both lose the dog and find a refuge.

The wound throbbed as he climbed, and when the lion reached a ledge high above the surrounding country he lay down on his left side to ease the pain. Hot anger set his brain on fire and he unsheathed and sheathed his claws. He had been hurt, and the knowledge that he dared not strike back infuriated him.

But he knew also that he need fear only as long as daylight lasted. Men were powerful then, but not when night came. The lion stretched out to let the winter sun warm him through his fur, and dozed. He had killed and fed on a deer the night before and was not hungry, and for two hours nothing disturbed him. Then at the foot of the cliff under his ledge, he heard Buck tonguing again.

The lion looked down at the hound, and angry lights flared in his eyes. Had he been sure that the dog was alone, the lion would have leapt down to offer battle. But he had laid one ambush for the red hound, and, quite unexpectedly, been shot at. The realization that a hunter could have been so close without the lion's knowing it was disturbing and he did not dare take another chance. With eyes and ears he searched intently the forest surrounding the base of the cliff. Though he couldn't see or smell him, it was possible that the hunter had followed the hound.

The lion rose, walked along the ledge, reared to draw himself onto a higher one, and kept climbing. All the while the bullet wound in his shoulder served as a painful reminder that men had again hurt him. Finally Buck's tonguing became faint in the distance, then ceased altogether. The red hound had lost the trail, at least temporarily.

Near the top of the bluff, the lion ran along a ledge where he offered no silhouette against the skyline, then he crawled over the bluff and started down the far slope. Night was coming; the rocks and boulders about him were encased in shadow as he went down into the forest. He was hungry again, so he crept into a thicket where deer were and slunk toward three does feeding in the twilight.

When the lion made his rush, a streak of pain seared his shoulder and brought a snarl to his lips. As he'd turned, he had twisted the wounded muscle. The resulting involuntary reaction delayed his rush just long enough to let the deer escape. Infuriated and sullen, the lion padded on until he found more game. He stalked and pulled down a half-grown buck, fed, then lay up in a thicket.

Dawn was just breaking when he heard Buck again tonguing on his trail. The lion rose from his comfortable bed, the end of his tail twitching resentfully. He wanted to wait and try to trap the hound again, but yesterday had both taught him a lesson and made him nervous. He had discovered that he could make mistakes. Turning, he took once more to the rocky bluffs where the dog could not follow, and spent the day sleeping on a ledge.

Night brought him down again, once more confident. Neither man nor man's dogs could make him do what he did not want to do while darkness covered him. So, when he again heard the hound on his trail, he did not run. Instead, he stood with one paw raised and head slanting backward while he listened. Then he turned completely around and crouched with his belly close to the snow.

This was what he had hoped would take place. Always before, when the dog found his trail, it had been during the day. The lion no longer dared try ambushing the hound in daylight; there was too much chance of being ambushed himself by a hunter. Now, even if there should be a hunter, the lion knew very well that there was almost no possibility of his being seen. He waited for the hound, his lips drawn back in a snarl.

Buck's deep voice awakened the night, and the tall rock bluffs sent the tones back in echoes from their craggy summits. The tonguing grew louder as the dog came nearer, and the lion tensed himself, waiting for the moment to strike. Presently he saw the hound, a flitting shadow black against the snow. The dog stopped.

They faced each other silently across the forty feet that separated them. Within the heart of each was vicious hatred for the other. The lion moved first.

He flashed across the short space as he would have rushed a deer. His actions were lightning-swift, but they were not as fast as they would have been had no wound hampered him. The lion's front paws came down on the place where the dog had been a split second before.

Buck twisted out of danger and bored in from the side, slicing at the lion's flank. His fangs ripped through skin into flesh. The lion slashed with a front paw, but where he had intended to deal the dog a crippling blow he succeeded only in knocking him sidewise. When the lion tried to follow up and pin the hound down, Buck rolled out of the way. He scrambled to his feet and faced his enemy.

They circled warily, each with a new respect for the other. The lion backed up until his rear was sheltered by a tree. He made a false rush and retreated back to his sheltering tree. That split second while the lion was moving gave Buck another opportunity to strike. He charged in, trying to slice the big tendon in the lion's rear leg. He succeeded only in biting out a mouthful of hair, and when the lion flashed at him he scooted sideways. The lion followed, twisting and turning as the dog dodged. Twice he came close to pinning the red hound.

In the trees overhead, a pine martin preened his fur and watched the battle. To one side a buck deer, wandering through the winter night, scented the lion and stood stock still in his tracks. Then he faded quietly into the forest.

The lion's rage was mounting to an almost insane fury. Twenty times he had tried to catch and kill the dog, and at no time had he succeeded in dealing more than a glancing blow. The bullet wound had slowed him and the hound was very fast. Desperately the lion tried again to catch and kill his tormentor but it was like trying to pin down a moving shadow. Every time he rushed, Buck dodged and came back for a counter strike, until the lion was torn in a half dozen places. He still wanted to continue the fight, but approaching daylight made him afraid.

The lion lunged again, and when he failed to catch the hound he kept on running. Buck nipping at his heels, he raced a hundred yards to a ledge of rocks. Over the top the lion deliberately slowed to a walk, for he knew that the hound could not climb up here. The lion stopped to look back and snarl, then went higher into the rocks.

His brain was on fire and the fury that engulfed him showed itself in his blazing eyes and twitching tail. He had wanted above all else to kill the hound, and failure to do so pitched his anger to the boiling point. The lion sought a high ledge and licked the numerous wounds Buck had inflicted. He looked from his resting place out across the rimrock. There was within him a great urge to kill, to strike and hurt the creatures he hated, and as the day passed that urge became unconquerable.

He left his lair while an hour of daylight remained and made a slow way into a canyon. The lion paused to listen for the hound, and continued on his way when he did not hear him. Night had fallen by the time he came to the road, and the lion stood for a long time in the sheltering darkness. Reassured, he padded down the asphalt highway, between the plow-thrown heaps of snow.

He knew all the ranches and houses along here, and had a definite destination. There were a dozen sheep penned in a stout board fence about a hundred yards from one ranch house, their only guardian a furry little dog. Nearing the ranch house, the lion leaped from the road into the yard. Wood smoke hung heavy in the air, but the lion had smelled that before and he was not afraid of it.

His nose told him that there were no people around. In one easy bound the lion cleared the stockade that fenced the sheep and was in among them. They ran crazily, bleating their terror, but there was no escape and the lion struck fast. The little furry dog came out of his kennel with a throaty growl, but could not get into the stockade.

It was over in a matter of seconds. When all the sheep lay dead inside their enclosure, the lion jumped back out and killed the little dog too. Then he ran across the road, was caught for a second in the headlights of an oncoming car, and fled into the protecting forest.

The car that caught the lion in its lights was driven by Bob Carew's mother. Bob and his father were in Gaston and she'd been visiting a friend who lived down the canyon. She saw the lion, but it was only a momentary shadow in the lights and at first she thought it was a deer. Finding food scarce, they often came at night to raid the ranch's haystacks. Parking the car, Mrs. Carew gave the supposed deer no second thought while she fumbled in her purse for the house key. Then she paused.

Their little dog was an affectionate creature and strictly a home lover. Almost never did he even leave the yard and he was always on hand to greet, with tail-wagging enthusiasm, any member of the family who came home. She realized that he was not there, and could not understand it.

"Brownie," she called.

When he did not respond, she entered the house and flicked a light on. Though there was not a great deal of traffic at this time of the year, it occurred to her that he might have strayed onto the road and been struck by a car. A flashlight in her hand, Mrs. Carew went back out on the porch.

There was no moon, but the sky was clear and the night had that translucent quality which is characteristic of many winter nights. About to go around the road, Mrs. Carew noticed an object lying midway between the house and the sheep pen. Flashing her light toward it, she saw the furry little body.

She was afraid but not panicky. A ranch wife, she was accustomed to the various emergencies that arise on an isolated ranch. Running to the little dog, she flashed her light on it, then saw lion tracks in the snow. Cautiously she went to the sheep pen.

After one look, she ran back to the house, took her husband's rifle from its rack, and got back into the car. Then she drove to the gravel road that cut off to Allis Torrington's house. Here she had to park her car, for snowplows never ran down the gravel. She would have to walk. Her flashlight shining about, the rifle clutched firmly, she walked slowly until she saw Allis's lights shining through frosty windows. Then she ran, and did not stop until she had burst in on the startled occupants.

"Mrs. Carew!" said Johnny, jumping up. "What's wrong?"

"I thought I'd better come here," she said. "My husband and Bob are in Gaston and I've been visiting. While all of us were away, a lion raided our ranch. He killed our twelve Suffolk sheep and the dog."

"How long ago?" Allis asked quickly.

"Not more than half an hour. I saw the lion cross the road when I drove in, but thought it was a deer until I found the dog and sheep, and saw lion tracks in the snow."

Allis began pulling on rubber pacs. "We'll be with you right away. Johnny, put the hounds on leashes."

Jacketed, carrying their rifles and with the dogs on short leashes, they hurried back up the gravel road and got into the car. Johnny quieted the three hounds in the rear seat while Mrs. Carew drove back down the plowed road. They parked in the ranch yard and Allis looked at the lion tracks carefully.

"It's the big one," he announced. "Cut 'em loose, Johnny."

As Johnny unsnapped the leashes, Allis said, "Take it!"

The three hounds cast, straightening out the trail. Then Major's thunderous roar echoed through the night. Doe and the bluetick joined in.

"Let 'em run a bit so we can get a line on where they're going," Allis said. "Are you afraid to stay alone, Mrs. Carew? I promise, he won't be back."

"I'm not afraid," she said firmly. "Just get that lion!"

Faint in the distance, another tonguing hound was

heard. Johnny and Allis looked at each other, startled. Coming nearer, the hound's baying increased in volume. Then there was a rush in the night and Buck swept past.

# 12

# The Ambush

When the lion left the Carew ranch he did not hurry, but loped along at a steady pace. He was no stranger in this area, and knew where he was going.

He splashed into the creek, ran a little way up it, jumped out, and quartered up a slope. When he reached the summit he turned to listen. Again he had dared strike and kill that which belonged to man, and he expected pursuit. But he was not afraid of it. He was not even disconcerted when he heard the hound pack on his trail.

Trotting a little way to a chasm, he jumped it. He knew that he could not lose the hounds this easily, because experience had taught him that they would find a way around. But he knew it would delay them.

He stopped again when the red hound's voice rang out. But though Buck had followed him relentlessly, he still did not worry. The same three hounds that had been on his trail before were on it again; he

173

recognized their voices. He also recognized the baying of the hound that had harassed him back and forth across the rimrock. But after the successful, though grueling, run he had already had ahead of the hound pack, the lion was confident of his ability to stay ahead of all four dogs.

He trotted along, not going fast enough to tire or even wind himself. He heard the three hounds reach the chasm he had leaped and yell their frustration because they could not cross. Then he heard the sound of Buck's voice catch up and blend with theirs. The baying of the hounds became faint in the distance and for a while the lion could not hear them at all.

Slowing to a walk, he moved silently across the snow-whitened rimrock and stopped when he came to a bluff. Here he stretched out to rest beside a young pine. Ten feet above him was a ledge, and above that more ledges and outcroppings. If necessary he could climb the bluff, but before he did that he wanted once more to try conclusions with this hound pack. The hounds were his mortal enemies. They had chased him and fought him. If he could, he would kill all of them.

An hour and a half later, having found a way around the chasm, the hounds were on him again. The lion rose with his back to the bluff, ready to meet them. He tensed himself, preparing to spring, but at the same time he felt a little uneasiness. Something was different.

When the hounds ran as a pack before, Major had always led them. Now the red hound ran well ahead of the rest. A throaty battle challenge rolled from his throat as he closed in for the fight. The lion backed until his rear brushed the bluff. As Buck rushed straight in, the lion calculated his strike. When the red hound was near enough he swiped with his paw, but he hit nothing.

The red hound was no longer there. He had slipped aside as swiftly as a darting swallow, and in a split second he was back in again. His slashing fangs sought the jaw, and sliced away a piece of the lion's flabby lip.

Now the other three hounds had come up. Major struck from one side, Doe and the bluetick from the other, while Buck whisked around to slash at the lion's rear. The lion whirled, intending to pin the red hound against the cliff. His striking paw collided with Buck's ribs, and the dog grunted as the wind was knocked out of him. But it was no more than a glancing blow. The red hound ferociously returned to the attack.

The lion's nervousness increased. After fifteen minutes of fighting the dogs, he sensed the futility of trying to catch them. He made a savage little rush that sent the hounds back, then turned and sprang easily to the ledge. Even as he leaped, Buck leaped with him and sliced through the loose skin on the big cat's belly.

The lion snarled in rage, looking down at the frantic hounds. It seemed an easy thing to jump upon and kill any one of them, but the lion had tried that before and he knew it was not easy. The hounds were too swift and wary to be pinned down. The lion licked blood from his torn lip, then curled his head around to soothe his torn belly with a warm tongue. He paced back and forth uneasily.

The breeze was strong in his face and presently, faint in his nostrils, he caught the scents of Johnny and Allis Torrington. The lion knew them both, for he had run across Johnny's trail up in the rimrock and Allis's at the house where he'd killed the calves and the two old dogs. When the lion was satisfied that these were the only two humans following the hounds, he turned and climbed the bluff.

It was high and very steep, with only narrow ledges which, in places, gave way to mere outjutting paw holds. The lion sprang from a ledge toward such an outcropping, fell back, and with catlike agility landed on the ledge again. He tried a second time, caught the outcropping with his front paws, and scrambled from there to another ledge. He ran along that to the top of the bluff.

The lion heard the hounds' tonguing cease as they left the bottom of the bluff to seek a way around it. He loped swiftly through a forest of stunted pines and for a while did not hear the hounds at all. But he was sure that they would come again. The lion came to another chasm and waited. He had a way to escape, but he wanted one more chance at the hounds before he took it. Presently he heard them.

The pack came nearer, and the lion tensed himself. This time Buck was a hundred and fifty yards ahead of Major, while Doe and the bluetick brought up the rear. The lion unsheathed and sheathed his claws.

As he had done before, the red hound came straight in. The lion waited, his tail twitching. But when Buck seemed within reach, and the lion struck, only the very tip of his paw brushed the red hound's ribs. The great curved claws tore away only a little hair.

Buck came back in, striking at the lion's neck. He missed the artery, but his teeth sliced through a vein and red blood spurted on the snow. In a spasm of fury, the lion threw caution to the winds and bounded wildly after his tormentor. Before he could pin the red hound, the rest of the pack came up. In his mad attempts to kill Buck, the lion had put twenty feet between the chasm and himself. He turned and raced for it while the hounds nipped at his sides and head. The lion sprang across the gap. Safe on the other side, he turned to face the dogs.

Fury seethed within him, and he snarled at the yelling pack. But because he knew they could not reach him at once, when he left he merely walked away. He crossed the top of a ridge and made his way into a canyon.

When he came to Horse Cleft, he entered it deliberately. The lion jumped the ledge, sniffed at the snow-covered body of Jake Kane, and turned to listen for the hounds. He could not hear them.

The lion sought a patch of dwarf cedar near the place from which he had ambushed Jake Kane and flattened himself there. He lay very quietly, knowing that he could not be seen. Except for Buck, the hounds could not get up here. If the red hound came, the lion could deal with him alone, then leap out of the cleft and climb the nearest bluff. If the hunters came, the lion was ready for them.

He wanted to settle another score.

For ten minutes after Buck ran past, Johnny and Allis Torrington remained in the ranch yard with Mrs. Carew. They heard the hounds pause momentarily where the lion had waded the creek, give tongue as they straightened out the trail, and pause again where the lion had jumped the chasm.

"He's treed!" Johnny exclaimed.

"No, he hasn't," Allis disagreed. "He's gone some place that the hounds can't and they're working on his trail. I reckon we'll go, Mrs. Carew."

"Shall I have Pete and Bob come help you after they get home?"

"Better not." Allis shook his head. "Give them another hour and those hounds will be a long ways in. Anybody will have a hard time finding them or us.

You might have 'em hit our trail in the morning, though, if they feel like it."

"Are you going to be out all night?"

"I think so. I don't see much chance of getting that lion in a corner tonight. He's just too smart. Oh say, can you loan us a flashlight? We left in such a hurry that I forgot one."

"Certainly." Mrs. Carew went into the house, got a big, multiple-cell flashlight, and gave it to Allis. "Here you are. The batteries are new; they've scarcely been used."

"Thanks."

In the distance, the hounds were still trying to find a way around the chasm and were still tonguing. Johnny fidgeted, wanting to be off on the hunt instead of standing here indulging in what seemed like useless conversation.

"Don't you think we'd better go?" he said pointedly.

"Keep your shirt on," Allis advised. "We've got some figuring to do."

"But the hounds are stopped and we could help them."

"The hounds can take care of themselves. Our job is to take care of the cat. Just remember that Jake Kane tried every trick he knew to get this lion and he didn't do it."

"What are we going to do?"

Allis said grimly, "Try to outguess that cat. I know he won't tree. If he would, Jake would have had him."

They crossed the road and started into the rimrock, their pace necessarily slow because Allis was too old to move fast. The tonguing hounds became silent, then began again. Their voices became fainter as they ran farther away. On a steep upward slope, Allis stopped to rest, and the sound of the hounds faded almost out of hearing.

Allis said, "That's as smart a cat as has ever run the rimrock, Johnny."

"That's saying a lot."

"But it's true. He knows how to leave a break in his trail and he doesn't panic. My idea is that he feels sure of himself because it's night, and he knows darn well that he can't be seen. I also suspect he'd like to trap the hounds. I think he hates them a lot more'n most lions do."

"Why should that be?"

"If I knew, I'd know a lot more about this lion than I do. I'm only guessing, but it's my idea that a hound pack treed him once and he got into a real mess. Maybe he was shot but only wounded and got away, or something like that. That's why he won't tree again. He knows what will happen if he does."

"How do you plan to get him?"

"If I've got him figured right, he won't push himself too hard tonight, feeling safe in the dark. That's one reason why Jake didn't get him. He just won't show himself in daylight. But in the morning he'll probably head for the nearest wild and broken country where he can hole up. We'll have to be somewhere near there when he comes or we'll lose him again. I think he'll look for a place where neither man nor hounds can reach him."

The wind keened around the peaks and played doleful tunes on frost-tautened branches of trees. There was the bawling of a lonely deer that had strayed out of its cedar canyon and become lost on the night-shrouded slopes. In a nearby snow tunnel a mouse squeaked. But the hounds were out of hearing.

Allis stopped to rest again and Johnny halted beside him. He felt some doubts. This was not the way he'd have run the hunt. Instead, he would have tried to follow the hounds; he did not believe that the lion would refuse to tree. But Allis was a hunter of vast experience and Johnny bowed to his superior wisdom.

The old man led the way down a slope, shone the flashlight on a brawling little stream so swift that it had not frozen, and walked across on rocks that thrust rounded backs out of the running water. He turned to light Johnny's way across, then snapped the light off and quartered up another slope.

Reaching the nose, where the slope pitched the other way, they suddenly heard the hounds very clearly. It was a wild, savage melody, all the more spine-tingling because of its discord. All four hounds were obviously at the same place. For a moment Allis and Johnny stood silently, overcome by the drama of what they were hearing and what their imaginations created.

Johnny whispered, "Sounds like a tree bark to me."

"No, he hasn't treed. There aren't any trees down there big enough for him to climb. I think the lion's fighting the dogs at some break. Listen!"

The voices of the hounds rose in frenzied crescendo, then faded to a few fretful barks. All was silent.

"What now?" Johnny asked.

"The dogs pushed him too hard and the lion got away. Probably jumped some chasm they couldn't."

"But they'll find the trail again?"

"Sure. Major will know how to do it, or that red hound will."

Allis led through the night, using his flashlight only where it was necessary. They came to a sheer-walled chasm and Allis swore softly.

"We can't cross here; darn thing's about two hundred feet deep. Come on."

They went on to where the chasm widened into a canyon. The walls were still steep, but there were protruding rocks to furnish footholds and small trees for hand grips. Allis used his flashlight until they were at the bottom of the canyon. Startlingly near, the thunder of the pack swelled in the night, then faded in the distance as the tonguing hounds swept along on the hot scent.

Johnny helped Allis on the hard climb out of the canyon, and both were panting when they finally reached the other rim. Their jackets hung open, and Johnny pushed his hat back on his perspiring head. He listened, but all he heard was the sighing of wind in the trees and the occasional cry of a night-prowling animal. Johnny wondered.

He knew only one way to hunt lions; follow the pack when they struck a trail and shoot the lion out of a tree, or wherever else it sought refuge, when the dogs bayed it. He looked wonderingly at his grandfather. If Allis's plan worked, then Johnny would know a great deal about hunting that he had never known before. But he doubted if the plan would succeed. Anticipating the next move of a lion, or any other wild creature, was not easy.

Just ahead was a tall peak known as Fire Chair because of the brilliant colors that glowed on it when the sun shone. There were only small trees on the sides of Fire Chair and nothing at all on the summit. Certainly no dog-driven lion would ever go there, but that was where Allis was heading.

"Are we going to climb Fire Chair?" Johnny asked.

"That's right."

Johnny said nothing. His grandfather must have his own reasons for climbing the peak. Supporting themselves against boulders and grasping the thin little pines that grew on Fire Chair's slopes, they climbed slowly. Johnny kept a careful eye on Allis, and when the old man stumbled he gave him a hand.

They mounted to the summit of Fire Chair and buttoned their jackets again. Even in the canyons the wind had been brisk, but up here it was violent, tearing viciously at the two standing on the peak. Johnny cradled his rifle in the crook of his arm and thrust his cold hands into his pockets. He thought he heard an animal move, and then realized that it was only the wind blowing through the broken rock.

He stood tense and expectant. Allis meant to outguess the lion. If the old man guessed wrong, then the chase might lead anywhere, and would mean going back, picking up the trail at the last point they could, and following it through. Johnny knew with a certainty he could not have explained that, if such a course proved necessary, they would lose this lion.

"What are you aiming to do?" Johnny asked anxiously.

"Get that lion. He's thrown the hounds off at least twice that we know of and probably other times. He isn't moving fast, but with daylight he's going to hole up. I think he'll pick a spot not too far from here, and this is the best place to hear the hounds."

The night wore on, but it seemed endless. Johnny stamped and jumped about to warm himself and touched his nose with a finger. He could feel sensation there, and knew it was not frozen. When slow, pale dawn filtered slowly over the rimrock it seemed so faint and unreal that, at first, Johnny didn't even notice it.

Suddenly he thought he heard a tonguing hound.

He strained, letting his jaw hang slack the better to listen. The wind was still whistling through and around the broken rock, and instead of a hound he might have heard only the wind. Then, faint and far-off but clear, there came the tonguing of the whole pack.

"There they are!" Allis exclaimed.

"I hear them!"

"Come on, Johnny! They're heading toward Dead Man's Wall! I'll bet that's where the lion is!"

In the graying morning, Johnny followed Allis down Fire Chair's slope. He let his grandfather choose the pace through pine forest at the foot of the peak, and then they were looking across at the forbidding rise of Dead Man's Wall.

Allis sought a sloping cleft that led down into the canyon, and the tonguing of the hounds rose to a feverish pitch as they ran down the slope. The lion had holed up somewhere, and judging from the hounds' yelling Johnny decided that he must have entered Horse Cleft. The dogs could have followed him into any other. They rounded a bend and saw Horse Cleft just ahead of them. The yelling pack was there, at the base of the first steep pitch, and Buck was already halfway up that.

Allis said quickly, "Get him down, Johnny!"

Johnny took a leash from his pocket, looped it over Buck's neck, and pulled the dog down, snarling fiercely. Hastily Johnny tied the other end of the leash to a tree and stepped aside as Buck lunged at him. Then the red hound strained forward, his tongue dangling and every breath audible as the tightening leash choked him. Buck paid no attention, but strove harder.

"He sure wants to tangle with that lion."

"The lion's cooked his goose!" Johnny exclaimed. "He's gone in but he hasn't come out, and this is the only way out!"

Allis said soberly, "I don't like it."

"Why not?"

"It doesn't add up. Any other lion might run into a blind canyon, but not this one. He's gone into Horse Cleft for his own reasons."

"Maybe this country's strange to him and he didn't know what he was getting into."

"Could be, but I still don't like it. Johnny, I'm a little shaky from all this running. You lift those three hounds up over the ledge and then cut that red hellion loose. Seems he can get up all by himself."

"If the dogs run him out of there, the most we'll get is a flying shot when he comes! He's ours if we can catch him in there! Let me go alone and track him!"

Allis said grimly, "No. Too dangerous."

"Grand Pop," Johnny pleaded, "you'd go in there if you could climb that ledge and you know it!"

Allis muttered, "You don't know lions like I do."

"Maybe not, but you'd never have been a hunter if you were afraid of your game! Neither can I!"

Allis hesitated a long time and looked at Johnny with troubled eyes. But there was understanding in his face.

"You'll be careful?"

"Very careful!"

"All right, but I'm giving you just two minutes. If you don't see him by that time, I'm turning the red hound loose."

Johnny climbed the ledge and found the lion's tracks in the snow on top of it. The hair on the back of his neck prickled as he saw the size of the track. Johnny slipped the safety catch on his rifle and followed them slowly.

A step at a time, stopping to look at everything, he went up Horse Cleft. A hundred yards ahead, near a big pine, was a patch of dwarf cedar. Johnny studied the cedar intently. He could see nothing there, and anyhow a lion would not normally hide in such a place. Probably he had gone into one of Horse Cleft's two caves.

Fifteen yards from the clump of cedar, Johnny halted. To the right, in a nest of boulders, he had seen motion. Johnny brought the rifle to his shoulder, but the motion was not repeated. It might have been a squirrel or rabbit. Or it might have been and still could be, the lion. Johnny gazed intently at the boulders. He could hear the yelling hounds, but it was as though they were a very long way off. There was no other sound in Horse Cleft.

He whirled as a sudden, throaty roar of fury exploded almost right beside him. The leash dangling from his neck, Buck rushed past and charged straight at a huge lion that had sprung from the cedars. For the barest fraction of a second, with two enemies to face instead of only one, the lion hesitated.

It was someone else, Johnny thought vaguely, and not himself at all, who aimed his rifle and squeezed the trigger. He saw hair flick squarely in the center of the lion's head. The great beast, like some huge mechanical toy whose spring was running down, took one slow step. He raised a paw to hit at Buck, but now there was no power behind the strike. The lion stiffened spasmodically and went limp in the snow.

Johnny heard Allis's frantic shout. "Johnny! Are you all right?"

Johnny called shakily, "I'm all right. I got him."

He seemed to have no strength, and collapsed to a limp sitting position in the snow. He saw the red hound go to the lion, sniff at him, then contemptuously scratch snow over the big cat. Turning, the dog started digging in the snow. Johnny saw what Buck wanted there, and did not interfere as the dog revealed Jake Kane's body. The dog looked at Johnny and back at Jake.

There was no savagery in his manner now and no viciousness. When he finally padded toward Johnny he came slowly, with hesitant steps. But his feud was ended and his duty done. He was free to be a dog again and choose a master.

The red hound lay down in the snow and licked Johnny's hand.

# ABOUT THE AUTHOR

JIM KJELGAARD's first book was *Forest Patrol* (1941), based on the wilderness experiences of himself and his brother, a forest ranger. Since then he has written many others—all of them concerned with the out-of-doors. *Big Red, Irish Red,* and *Outlaw Red* are dog stories about Irish setters. *Kalak of the Ice* (a polar bear) and *Chip, the Dam Builder* (a beaver) are wild-animal stories. *Snow Dog* and *Wild Trek* describe the adventures of a trapper and his half-wild dog. *Haunt Fox* is the story both of a fox and of the dog and boy who trailed him, and *Stormy* is concerned with a wildfowl retriever and his young owner. *Fire-Hunter* is a story about prehistoric man; *Boomerang Hunter* about the equally primitive Australian aborigine. *Rebel Siege* and *Buckskin Brigade* are tales of American frontiersmen, and *Wolf Brother* presents the Indian side of "the winning of the West." The cougar-hunting *Lion Hound* and the greyhound story, *Desert Dog,* are laid in the present-day Southwest. *A Nose for Trouble* and *Trailing Trouble* are adventure mysteries centered around a game warden and his man-hunting bloodhound. The same game warden also appears in *Wildlife Cameraman* and *Hidden Trail,* stories about a young nature photographer and his dog.

# JIM KJELGAARD

In these adventure stories, Jim Kjelgaard shows us the special world of animals, the wilderness, and the bonds between men and dogs. *Irish Red* and *Outlaw Red* are stories about two champion Irish setters. *Snow Dog* shows what happens when a half-wild dog crosses paths with a trapper. The cougar-hunting *Lion Hound* and the greyhound story *Desert Dog* take place in our present-day Southwest. And, *Stormy* is an extraordinary story of a boy and his devoted dog. You'll want to read all these exciting books.

| | | | |
|---|---|---|---|
| ☐ | 15456 | A NOSE FOR TROUBLE | $2.50 |
| ☐ | 15368 | HAUNT FOX | $2.25 |
| ☐ | 15434 | BIG RED | $2.95 |
| ☐ | 15324 | DESERT DOG | $2.50 |
| ☐ | 15286 | IRISH RED: SON OF BIG RED | $2.50 |
| ☐ | 15427 | LION HOUND | $2.95 |
| ☐ | 15339 | OUTLAW RED | $2.50 |
| ☐ | 15365 | SNOW DOG | $2.50 |
| ☐ | 15388 | STORMY | $2.50 |
| ☐ | 15466 | WILD TREK | $2.75 |

**Prices and availability subject to change without notice.**

☐ **THE OWLSTONE**            15349/$2.50
**CROWN**
by X. J. Kennedy
When Timothy and Verity Tibbs follow a tiny ladybug private eye over a moon-lit path to Other Earth, magical adventures happen fast.

☐ **BONES ON BLACK**        15443/$2.25
**SPRUCE MOUNTAIN**
by David Budbill
Thirteen-year-olds Danny and Seth set out to explore Black Spruce Mountain because they love camping out. But Black Spruce Mountain appears to be haunted and their adventure is more than they bargained for.

☐ **SNOWSHOE TREK TO**      15469/$2.25
**OTTER RIVER**
by David Budbill
David and Seth have a lot in common besides their age. They share a love of adventure and specifically, they share a love of camping and exploring. And what better place to explore than the backwoods of Vermont?

☐ **CHRISTOPHER**             15363/$2.25
by Richard M. Koff
On a dare from a friend, Christopher knocks on the door of a haunted house. There he meets the "Headmaster" who teaches him how to release the amazing powers of his own mind.

# FROM THE SPOOKY, EERIE PEN OF
# JOHN BELLAIRS . . .

☐ **THE CURSE OF THE**　　　　15429/$2.75
**BLUE FIGURINE**

Johnny Dixon knows a lot about ancient Egypt and curses and evil spirits—but when he finds the blue figurine, he actually "sees" a frightening, super-natural world. Even his friend Professor Childermass can't help him!

☐ **THE MUMMY, THE WILL**　　　15323/$2.50
**AND THE CRYPT**

For months Johnny has been working on a riddle that would lead to a $10,000 reward. Feeling certain that the money is hidden somewhere in the house of a dead man, Johnny goes into his house where a bolt of lightening reveals to him that the house is not quite deserted . . .

☐ **THE SPELL OF THE**　　　　15357/$2.50
**SORCERER'S SKULL**

Johnny Dixon is back, but this time he's not teamed up with Dr. Childermass. That's because his friend, the Professor, has disappeared!

☐ **THE AGAINST TAFFY**                     15413/$2.50
**SINCLAIR CLUB**
by Betsy Haynes
It was bad enough when Taffy Sinclair was just a pretty face.
But now she's gone and developed a figure! This calls for
drastic measures from the Against Taffy Sinclair Club made
up of Jana Morgan and her four fifth-grade friends.

☐ **TAFFY SINCLAIR**                        15417/$2.50
**STRIKES AGAIN**
by Betsy Haynes
It is time gorgeous Taffy Sinclair had a little competition.
That's what Jana and her friends decide to give her when
they form a club called The Fabulous Five. But when the
club's third meeting ends in disaster, Jana finds she has four
new enemies!

☐ **TAFFY SINCLAIR,**                       15330/$2.50
**QUEEN OF THE SOAPS**
by Betsy Haynes
What could be worse? The snooty but perfectly gorgeous
Taffy has done it again—she's won a part in a soap opera to
play a beautiful girl on her deathbed. Nothing like this ever
happens to Jana Morgan or her friends, and they're not going
to stand being upstaged one more time!

# WITTY ADVENTURES BY
# FLORENCE PARRY HEIDE books

☐ **BANANA TWIST**                    15258/$2.25

Jonah D. Krock and Goober Grube are not the best of friends. In fact, they're not friends at all. But funny things can happen that turn an uneasy rivalry into a wacky friendship.

☐ **BANANA BLITZ**                    15258/$2.25

Jonah D. Krock can hardly wait to get to the Fairlee School, which boasts a TV and a refrigerator *in every room*! But Jonah's in for a surprise when his "new roommate turns out to be his old arch-rival Goober Grube!

☐ **TIME FLIES!**                     15370/$2.50

Noah is not looking forward to the birth of the new baby; he is convinced that babies only cry and scream and dribble— and they never help with the chores! But when the baby accidentally brings a $200.00 prize, Noah decides the baby isn't so bad after all.

# Shop at home
# for quality childrens books
# *and save money, too.*

Now you can order books for the whole family from Bantam's latest listing of hundreds of titles including many fine children's books. *And* this special offer gives you an opportunity to purchase a Bantam book for only 50¢. Here's how:

By ordering any five books at the regular price per order, you can also choose any other single book listed (up to $4.95 value) for just 50¢. Some restrictions do apply, so for further details send for Bantam's listing of titles today.